DINNER PARTY

Philip Garrard

ISBN: 0995558728
ISBN 13: 9780995558724

CHAPTER ONE

Jessica loved to wander through her garden every evening in the summer months. The flowers and shrubs looked at their best as the light began to fade, and the greenness of the grass seemed to take on an extra freshness - especially when the lawn had been cut that morning. Jess inspected every plant and blade of grass until she was satisfied that things were in order. It was probably an exaggeration to say that she scrutinised everything in this way, but her obsession with structure, order and image had led her family recommending, in no uncertain terms, that she visit a counsellor to get some help. Jess, however, didn't see it that way, proclaiming that she was merely paying attention to detail. The problem was that such attention took up most of her time during the day. Nor was it restricted to the garden. Her obsession with housework, cleaning, washing and cooking (and then cleaning again) was almost legendary in the neighbourhood. Sure, she was good at entertaining but the time she spent on preparation and, after everyone had left, cleaning up, meant she had little time for anything else. She sometimes sacrificed her sleep if her oven was still unclean after several scrubs following a dinner party.

Jessica Garnett was 35 years old, tall, blonde and reasonably attractive. She came from a good family who'd managed a farm in Wiltshire. From an early age she was encouraged to do well in anything she applied herself to. Consequently, she excelled at school and then university. She was very ambitious, but only to the extent of achieving her end goals. These were: detached house in the suburbs, big garden, successful husband, two cars, three holidays per year and two children. She had achieved all this by the age of 34 and had got to the stage where, apart from engaging in her daily maintenance regime, wanted everybody to know how well she'd done.

Her meek and mild husband, Andrew was an accountant by profession and had run his financial services business for about 10 years. He was subservient by nature as far as his dealings with his wife were concerned – she was by far the more dominant partner. However, he was a different person when it came to running an enterprise which provided creative tax avoidance solutions for his eighty or so clients. He was very good at this and, some would say, ruthless in arguing his case on behalf of his clients at court. As soon as he got home, however, he was submissive to Jess and raised little objection to her many instructions which ranged from mowing the lawn twice on Saturdays to giving her breakfast in bed on a daily basis. She controlled him at the weekends and while he was away at work she could concentrate on her obsessions, leaving the nanny, Olga, to look after the kids. He'd resigned himself to his lot and was quite happy to be bossed around at home. However, he was a caring man and although Jess didn't seem to care too much about her children, he did, and would take every opportunity to be with them, whether taking them to the park or browsing the computer for new electronic toys.

So there we have it. A near perfect family unit living near Wimbledon Village with easy access to the common which afforded great opportunity during the tennis season for entertaining friends and relatives allowing Jess to excel in her culinary skills; not to mention her mastery in presentation and her genius in small-talk. She was, in a sense, the envy of the neighbourhood –both men and women admired her. On the other hand, there were some who loathed what they regarded as her arrogant manner as, despite her many qualities, Jess never acknowledged that she could ever be wrong. Her way or the highway compounded by a stubbornness that often bordered on rudeness. Yes, Jess was the perfect hostess – although she did have her enemies.

She was a recognisable figure in the village and could often be seen drinking coffee with her friends during summer mornings after the rush hour traffic had dissipated, and the first signs of normal life rekindled and settled in for the rest of the day. Such was the routine of the day until about 3 pm when the traffic, beginning with the school run, started building up again.

It was on one of those summery mornings in July 2005 that she first had the idea. This was prompted during discussions with the coffee set – all women in their thirties and forties – on the subject of school reunions. They had all assembled at a coffee house which overlooked the common, and managed to secure a table which had been covered with a tastefully decorated plastic cloth. This displayed flowers and birds and reminded Jess of a restaurant she had visited recently in Northern France. There were four ladies in all - Jess, Joy, Martha and June – all very comfortable, all very suburbia. Some would say all very stuck up. The conversation soon turned to their favourite subject – the opposite sex:

Joy, a forty something personal trainer for the over fifties, mentioned how she had a crush on a boy in the upper sixth:

'He had longish brown hair, glasses and a big nose' she said 'but he was gorgeous and I couldn't take my eyes off him. He was in the school play. I remember as if it were yesterday. He played some sort of knight – I think his name was Hotspur – it was a Shakespearian history and he had to sword fight without his glasses. He cut such a dashing figure that I instantly fell in love with him.'

'Oh Joy' said Martha, a young mother and born again Christian living alone but strongly subsidised by her very rich parents, 'you are a dark horse. I didn't think men bothered you in that way.'

'Look Martha, when push comes to shove, I can fall in love with a man, just as I've fallen in love with many women in the past.'

They all laughed as Joy was well known for her promiscuity within the community and often boasted about her conquests in the gym – both male and female. She was unmarried and lived alone in a prestigious apartment on Wimbledon Hill. She was small, voluptuous, sexy and fit. She had a twinkle in her eye.

'What about you Jess' asked June, the fourth member of the gang who was a happily married lecturer in human biology, 'did you have any romances at school?'

'Funny you should say that June. I was just thinking the other day about my university days. I had plenty of relationships but none that really rocked my boat. There were a small group of us in a shared flat. We all got on marvellously well. I can still remember their names. We kept in touch. There was Natalie who studied geography – she now works for the Civil Service. There was Julia who's now, I think, a primary school teacher, and then there were the two guys, Othman and Nigel – they became policemen. I had a bit of a fling with Nigel but nothing came of it. They were great guys and excelled in everything – sport, partying, womanising – the whole lot. I've still got their email addresses.'

'You should have a reunion Jess' said Martha 'I went to one of those last year and met up with all my old school friends. It was a real hoot. It's amazing how some people just don't change; they don't move on and simply settle down into a mundane existence.'

'What all of them?' asked Joy.

'No, not all of them, some, like myself, became very successful and have made an exciting life for themselves.'

The other three thought to themselves that if it hadn't been for Martha's parents she would, by now, be in the gutter. However, they kept those thoughts to themselves.

'Yes, I know the feeling' said Jess. 'I like to think, as you know, that I've become rather successful. I mean, just look around, we're able to live in one of the best suburbs in London, drink coffee at our leisure and discuss past relationships'.

'You're right of course' said June 'but don't you sometimes wish you had more? I'm happily married to Luke – nothing could be better – but sometimes I want my comfortable life to be spiced up a bit?'

'What, you mean you want an affair?' asked Jess.

'Of course not silly. Luke is great in bed. He's kind and considerate...'

'And rich' Joy interrupted.

'Money's not everything Joy. When I say spicing it up I don't necessarily mean an affair. I'm sure Luke would be devastated if I had one. I mean doing something different like climbing Kilimanjaro.'

'You can keep your mountains June' said Jess. 'I wouldn't mind having an affair provided it didn't upset things.'

'What do you mean' asked June.

'Well, in France, it's quite normal for the husband to have a mistress. The wife may not be happy about it but feels secure because she knows, provided he gets his freedom, that is, his bit on the side, the marriage is intact and normality, whatever that is, prevails. That arrangement doesn't rock the boat, so why can't it work the other way round?'

'And what about the Mormons' Joy piped up. 'The husband can have more than one wife. It follows, in this world of equal opportunity, that us women should be allowed more than one lover. What's right for men should be right for women. Of course, it doesn't bother me one way or the other as I'm single and can have my pick of any man or, for that matter, any woman.'

The four of them burst into laughter as they realised how the topic of conversation always seemed to degenerate to sex. Jess laughed the loudest as she was having an affair with June's husband, Luke. He was everything Andrew wasn't – commanding, handsome and an all-round brute. Yes, of course she loved her husband, children and, indeed the whole set up, but her life wasn't complete. She was given sufficient freedom to indulge her compulsive obsessions – she loved the structure and order of her life – but she needed a little light relief now and again to relieve the disciplined life she led. Luke gave her that relief and, despite her occasional pangs of guilt, Jess was not going to let anyone destroy the perfect set up. What people didn't know didn't worry them. That's how structure and order were maintained in a civilised society. That was her philosophy – keep momentum, maintain control and preserve status – at all costs.

'On the question of a reunion' Jess said 'you've given me an idea. I'd love to see my old university mates again and what better way to do this than invite them to one of my dinner parties. I could really go to town and prepare a five course menu with an option for vegetarians.'

'But there might not be a vegetarian amongst them?' pointed out Martha.

'That wouldn't matter. I would prepare one any way – to show how flexible and tolerant I'd become. There would be pre dinner drinks of course – the best champagne and Pimms for those who can't stomach the bubbly stuff. There would be all sorts of canapés, caviar and oysters...wait a minute, I've got an even better idea... I could invite them individually without telling them who else will be there. I'd tell them to wear a mask (which I would provide of course) so that when they arrived it would be a mystery as to who was who. I could wear my swan mask.'

'Your swan mask?' Joy asked.

'Yes. I've got a white mask come head cover with a swan's head attached to it.'

'But wouldn't that wobble about?' asked June.

'Of course it would. But that would add to the humour and show how I'd developed a keen and unique wit since uni days.

'What other masks have you got Jess?' asked Martha.

'I've got a whole selection. A wolf of course. A cat, a Saddam Hussein...em, a rabbit, a mouse. You name it I've got it. We had a masquerade ball about two years ago for friends and relatives so I've got hundreds.'

'How come we weren't invited?' joked June.

'Don't be silly June – you're my Wednesday morning coffee friends – I have to draw the line somewhere.'

'Well thanks' said Martha ' I suppose you've a set of coffee friends for each day of the week?'

'More or less sweetie. But that's what life is all about in the village – having a wide circle of friends... any way they'd all turn up in their masks and, at the appropriate moment, I would ask them to reveal themselves.'

'But you'd probably recognise their voices and mannerisms before the unveiling' said Martha.

'Probably, but that wouldn't matter... I would have to provide masks for their partners of course.'

'Wouldn't it be better to restrict the party to your uni mates – the partners may find it a bit boring because you guys would just be talking about the good old days' said June.

'True, but then again, I'm sure they would all want to nose around, especially the women. It would give them all a chance to see the house and garden.'

'And the Bentley which, I assume, will be parked outside the garage so they can gauge your status immediately they drive on to the forecourt' said Joy.

'Exactly.'

CHAPTER TWO

Luke Masterson, husband of June and a bit of rough on the side for Jessica, was born in Hackney, East London, but was brought up and schooled in Buckhurst Hill, Essex. He did well at school, but learnt his trade on the streets. As a youngster he demonstrated a natural skill for enterprise and profit. For example he would find an old bike abandoned in the road, renovate and sell it to either one of his mates or a stranger who was passing by. Anything he saw, from trainers to mobiles, represented, for him, a chance to make money and, having *The Micawber Principle* instilled in him at an early age, made him wary of debt and fearful of the lure of the dreaded credit card. Consequently, as he grew older, he was never in debt and, apart from the mortgage, remained in total control of his finances. However things changed as he became greedier as we shall see.

Eventually he got himself a job as a trader on the Stock Exchange, met June, got married and lived in relative luxury in the posh end of Raynes Park (known as West Wimbledon). Through his desire for money he'd taken up gambling in his mid twenties, moving on to drug dealing in his thirties. Unbeknown to June he led a double life. He had connections with suppliers in the East End of London and sold drugs to the many contacts he had in the city. He managed to completely separate these activities from his domestic life. As far as June knew Luke was a trader and nothing more. He also had time to operate a number of affairs. His latest conquest was Jessica with whom he had been having sex for the last six months.

Luke was tall, handsome, intelligent and an all-round bad boy. He wore his hair very short and sported a designer, closely shaven, beard. Every week morning he worked out in the city gym before the markets opened at 8 am. June, oblivious to his extra –curricula activities, was very much in love with him and never quizzed him when he arrived home late. When she did, he always had a satisfactory explanation, pointing out the pressures of working life and the many risks he'd taken to maintain the standard of living she had become accustomed to.

On the following Wednesday afternoon, after the coffee morning meeting, he'd managed to get time off to meet Jess at their secret rendezvous – a holiday inn in Sutton, about seven miles south of Wimbledon. Jess was able to finish her chores by 3 pm and could rely on Olga to look after the children when they came home from school. Her usual excuse was that she wanted a new outfit for the weekend and wanted to shop around in the local area.

They met at around 3.30 pm and after some passionate love making rolled off each other to gaze at the ceiling.

'That was good.' Jess said trying to catch her breath. 'You're like a locomotive.'

'That's me. Once I start, I can't stop.'

'Are you like this with June?'

'Don't ask Jess, that's another life.'

'How many lives have you got?'

'I've got a few but nothing for you to worry about.'

'I'm not worried. I couldn't care less how many lovers you've got. I get what I want from you and that's all I really care about.'

'How romantic. It's not all about sex you know.'

'It is for me as far as you're concerned Luke. You give me what I want. It's dead boring at home and apart from my flair for socialising, I've got nothing much to look forward to.'

'What about your kids and the whole domestic scene.'

'What about it? I've cracked that and need something new.'

'Like what?'

'A new experience. Something I've never done before.'

There was a pause in the conversation as Luke considered what Jess had just said.

'Perhaps I could help you, although you'll have to pay.'

'What are you talking about Luke?'

'Have you ever tried cannabis?'

'Of course not. I'm not into drugs.'

'But cannabis isn't a hard drug. A lot of people take it for medicinal purposes. It'll give you a buzz and help you find what you're looking for.'

'Stop right there lover boy, I'm not interested... but how do you get hold of the stuff?'

'It's a long story. Some years ago I got myself into a little bit of trouble. I met a guy at the Stock Exchange. His name was Grant O'Malley. He was a big guy with tattoos and no neck. But he was smart, gutter smart and made lots of money through fluctuations in the exchange rates. He was a natural trader. He came from a travelling background and was brought up in a traditional gypsy family. By the age of eighteen he was bare knuckle fighting in all the local tournaments within the Irish fraternity. These were all illegal, of course, but he won a lot of prize money which he spent wisely on his education – trader education. Through a number of contacts he got himself a job on the Stock Exchange and, identifying me as some kind of rival, struck up a relationship after a few beers in the Royal Exchange. He told me about his family and how poor they were. He reckoned that when he was young, to save money, his brothers and himself had to share the same underpants until they were worn out. His mother would then nick another set from a washing line to avoid the expense of buying new ones. Looking back on that conversation I realise now that what he told me was a load of blarney – absolute bullshit – but I believed him at the time.'

'Where's this all going Luke, I've got to get back to the house.'

'I know, I know, but let me finish. Any way we struck up a relationship and spent many evenings getting pissed. As I said, he was a good trader and kept his job even though he was out of his head a lot of the time.'

'What do you mean?'

'Well, it wasn't just the booze, it was the drugs that were screwing up his mind. He'd met a drug gang in Bethnal Green and became a dealer. He made lots of sales in the city and suggested I get involved.'

'What do you mean?'

'He would sell small bulks to me and I would sell to my contacts in Essex and anywhere else to those who were interested.'

'And your point?'

'The point is that, over the years, I've consumed more drugs than I've sold and now I owe Grant.'

'But you're making enough money on the Exchange to counter any debt?'

'Not really. I've not been too successful recently and I'm out of cash. The fact is I'm living on credit cards and unbeknown to June, we're in serious debt.'

'So you're hooked on drugs?'

'I wouldn't say that. If I can sell to you, that would help matters. Yes I'm a bit hooked but nothing I can't handle.'

'You don't come across pissed.'

'I'm not. I just take enough to get permanently high.'

'I don't know what that means Luke but I'm not getting involved in illegal drugs. I f you need a loan, I'll help you out. But I'll want my money back.'

Again there was a pause in the conversation as Luke considered his next move.

'But you're looking for an adventure, a new experience. I'll guarantee you'll get a high that will alter your whole life – in a good way of course. You've never tried drugs so why not give it a try?'

'No Luke. Leave me out. How much money do you need?'

'About 20k.'

'What?'

'20k'

'I can't afford that. You need to kick your habit, if that's what you're telling me, and sort out your problems. Does June know anything about this?'

'Of course not. She lives in another world - and I want to keep it that way.'

'Sorry Luke. Can't help out. It's too risky. I don't mind having my bit on the side but I don't want to get involved in any drug wars'.

'It's not a drug war. It's simply that I owe Grant a few grand and, at the moment, I don't know where I'm going to get the money from.'

'Look Luke. I'll think about it. I don't want to lose you, but at the same time, I don't want any complications. You can understand that can't you?'

'Sure, but I thought I was doing you a favour? Now that I've told you about my problems, I was hoping that you would help me out?'

'It doesn't work like that darling. Sure I like a bit of fun but don't forget I'm a happily married woman with too much to lose. You are on your own on this one Luke.'

'Thanks Jess. Thanks a million.'

At that Luke got out of bed and went to the bathroom to take a leak. He was clearly in a mood. Jess watched his nicely formed arse as he disappeared around the corner of the bedroom. She thought she had it made. Luke had a fantastic body and an income, so she'd thought up to now, which would keep one of her best mates happy. But she didn't like the criminal background, nor the fact that he owed someone, who seemed to be quite influential, a lot of money, which if he didn't pay up, would probably end up in the rearrangement of his face. She hesitated and then said:

'Okay Luke. Let me check my expenses out. I'll give you a call. Now, I've got to get home.'

'Thanks Jess.'

They both got dressed and Luke noticed the beautiful contours of Jess's body. She was not the best looking girl on the block, but boy, was she sexy. She had long blond hair which had obviously been coloured bearing in mind her age, but it was thick and curly, reaching down to the top of her bottom. Her bottom was a piece of *Botichellian* art: rounded, big, and yet taut and muscular – a voluptuous pear with a crack running down the centre. Any man would want to get between those cheeks!

As she approached the door she turned round to Luke, who was sitting on the sofa having washed and shaved, and waved him goodbye saying that she would phone him tomorrow after she'd established how much money she could lend him. Luke blew her a kiss, slipped his shoes on and rang June on his mobile:

'Hi June, on my way home.'

'Wow, you're early. What's up?'

'Oh nothing much, no more deals to be made, so I thought I'd get home early to see my lovely wife.'

'That's nice. Can't wait to see you.'

'Nor me.'

'Oh, and one last thing – I hope you're in the mood for 'rumpy pumpy', I've been thinking about it all day.'

'I'll be in the mood – don't you worry about that my darling. See you later.'

The following day Jess phoned Luke and explained that she'd reconsidered her position and couldn't help him financially after all. The fact of the matter was that she had very little in her personal account and the risk of transferring money from the joint account – and having to explain the transfer to her husband - was not a risk she was prepared to take.

She also thought it best for everybody concerned, including her best friend June, that their affair should end immediately.

'It will be your loss in the end Jess. You're not getting any younger and those beautiful tits of yours will soon be pointing south.'

'That's the chance I'm willing to take. Sure, I find you attractive but, as I've said before, I don't won't anything to upset my nice little life. Your revelations have complicated what, up to now, has been a straightforward situation. We both liked a bit on the side but this had to be without strings. Your involvement with drugs and your need to pay off your debts using me as your creditor, is a step too far. It will get messy and I don't do messy. I like order and structure. I want out and that's the end of it. It was nice while it lasted, but now it's over.'

'Okay Jess. I get the picture. Thanks for leaving me in the shit. I hope you can sleep at night when they find me dead in the gutters.'

'Oh don't be so melodramatic Luke, and don't put that one on me. I'm not the guilty party here. You got involved with drugs, not me. You got yourself in debt through illegal practices so you have to sort yourself out. I'm sorry, but this is goodbye.'

Jess put the phone down and never saw Luke again.

CHAPTER THREE

Inspector Nigel Francis opened his eyes and woke up to a world of pain. His head was about to burst having spent longer in the pub then he'd antici- pated. They were celebrating the sergeant's fiftieth and after three pints of strong lager Nigel, for some inexplicable reason, decided to embark upon the vodka. This was a mistake and he was now paying for his sins. He didn't remember getting into bed but around about 4 am he did remember being sick on the carpet. He must have lost consciousness after that because the next thing he knew, he was wak- ing up to pain. Never again, he thought to himself. Thank God he's got the morning off.

He slowly got up and realised he was still fully clothed. He'd been sick down his front as well as on the floor. He was too ill to clean it up so he struggled to the bathroom and popped two paracetamols down his throat. He then cupped a mouthful of water from the cold tap, stripped off and lay naked on the bathroom floor. He then kept repeating to himself 'never again' until he rediscovered the land of nod.

After what seemed like minutes he woke up and was surprised to discover that he'd been asleep for about two hours. The time was now 11 am and the pain had subsided. Thank God he said to himself and ventured out towards the kitchen. He returned to the bedroom with a bowl of hot water, sponges, cloths and kitchen towels. After clearing up his mess he was ready for a shower and decided to spend the next ten minutes standing very still in the cubicle letting the water, alternating between hot and cold, fall on his head in the hope that it would flush away the remains of his headache. It kind of worked which allowed him to wash the rest of his body, grab a towel and make his way to the kitchen where he made a cup of coffee and swallowed down two slices of bread – he didn't have time to toast them as he wanted an instant remedy to nullify his growing nausea.

He put on his underpants and lay on the sofa. As he did so he heard the postman push the mail through his letterbox and ring the front door. He wanted to get up but couldn't be bothered. He went back to sleep. After what seemed an eternity the phone rang and his old buddy Othman asked how he was:

'Terrible Oth. I don't remember a thing.'

'Well, I'm here to remind you. But before I do have you got your mobile and wallet? You'd better check. I'll wait.'

Nigel got off the sofa and found his abandoned clothes in the bathroom. He couldn't even remember taking them off. He went through his pockets and thankfully found all his possessions intact.

'Yep. All there. Now tell me what happened.'

'There's not much to tell. After about ten vodkas you fell asleep. One minute you were shouting and balling about the size of officer Wilson's bottom – not a good move – the next minute you were out for the count. It was as if you were making your final speech before surrendering to oblivion. We then got you home, found your keys and left you on your bed to die.'

'Oh dear, I guess a few apologies are due?'

'Don't worry, Linda took it quite well. She could see you were totally out of it.'

'Thank God for that. What about you, how are you Oth?'

Chief Inspector Othman, a Sudanese policeman, had been seconded to the Met following his capture of an MI5 operative's murderer in Cairo and his subsequent role in bringing down a rogue operative who, coincidentally, also worked for MI5. The Uk Government thought it would be a good idea to get Othman on side as it believed he knew too much about the murder of the eminent MI5 scientist, Dr Rob Williams. Othman was convinced that the Government was behind this murder although it had never been proved. Having said that Othman was regarded as a potential threat and so the Government suggested, as part of its desire for control, that he work alongside his mate, Inspector Francis, in support of the good old Metropolitan Police Force, or Service as the politicians prefer to call it. Amidst all this skulduggery and at the behest of Nigel, Othman unwittingly faked his own death only to re emerge once things had settled down. Subsequently, Othman got a call from Nigel with the suggestion of secondment which Othman gladly agreed to. Consequently, he'd been working in London for the last six months and planned to continue his stay for as long as he could.

'I'm okay. The other thing I'm phoning you about is Jessica Garnett – your old flame at uni.'

'My God I'd forgotten about her, although she does try to keep in touch.'

'Have you checked your post this morning?'

'Of course not. I'm seriously under the weather.'

'Well go to your front door and see if a package has been left on your step.'

Nigel got up and felt the pangs of a returning headache. He swayed a bit but then gathered momentum thus energising his legs into action. He walked steadily towards the passage while using the walls for support. He still hadn't recovered – never again he said to himself for the tenth time. He opened his front door and saw a package on the step. He took it inside and, without thinking, opened the package with a carving knife. The contents surprised him:

'It's some kind of hat. Wait a minute it's a wolf's head.'

'Put it on.'

'What?'

'Put it on your head and look at yourself through the peep holes.'

Nigel did what he was instructed and stared at himself in the mirror. He was wearing a wolf's head. He went back to the phone.

'Is this some kind of joke Oth?'

'It's a mask you idiot. Now go and read your emails.'

'Okay. Hold on.'

Nigel logged on to his computer and looked at his latest emails through the peep holes (he was still wearing his mask/hat). There was a message from Jessica which was sent yesterday. It read:

Hi Nigel

Hope you are well. Have decided to have a university reunion – a dinner party round mine. There will be others there but I want everybody to wear a mask so we don't know who's who. I want everybody to put on a funny voice so we can't tell who you are. At the right time we'll all take off our masks (I suppose it will be obvious who I am because I'll be the 'hostess with the mostess.' Still, it will give me a chance to show off my mask!). Please come. It will be held on 5th August at my home address. This is 16 Leicester Drive, Wimbledon Village. It's very near the high street so you won't miss it. Get here for seven. We can talk about the old times. It will be a hoot.

Apart from the mask, dress is smart casual.

Can't wait to catch up with the gossip.

See you soon

Love
Jess

Nigel returned to the phone

'I don't believe it Oth. Is this a wind up?'

'I don't think so Nige. I got the same message and a gorilla's mask in the post.'

'Are you going to go?'

'Why not. As Jess says it will be a hoot'.

'Yes, but as you know, Jess has always been a bit of a nutter. God knows what will happen. She'll probably go naked thinking we won't recognise her behind the mask.'

'You should know what she looks like Nige. You did go out with her.'

'Yeah, but not for long. I was happy that we parted company even though we continued to live in the same digs.'

'Yes, I remember. It was a little strained after that but we all got on in the end.'

'Do you think she's just invited our flat mates?'

'I expect so. Unless her house is the size of Buckingham Palace, I doubt whether she'll invite more than about ten. Having said that, who knows? With Jess you can never tell. On one hand she was obsessed with cleaning the flat, on the other she was getting blind drunk and randy. You could never predict her moods.'

'Too right. I pity her husband if she's got one. Talk about high maintenance – Jess was always hard to manage... anyway, got to go ... got a hangover to nurse. See you tomorrow buddy.'

Nigel arrived on time the following day. He was on the early shift which meant he would probably bump into Othman later that morning. The office was buzzing. There were officers catching up with paperwork while others, like members of the surveillance team, were making last minute checks on their equipment. There'd been a recent tip off regarding a drug gang working in the Bethnal Green area and news of a shipment – by way of a stolen Eddie Stobart lorry – arriving in a warehouse located on some wasteland behind *The Artful Dodger* pub. Surveillance, through their sources, had identified and tagged the lorry and the team were taking position for this afternoon's undercover operation.

Both Nigel and Othman were going to take part in the ambush – Nigel because he was the lead detective, and Othman to observe and support as necessary. There were four other armed plain clothes policemen who'd already taken up position in strategic spots around the warehouse. The officers on the ground would be in constant liaison with the surveillance team operating at both HQ and on site in a side street running adjacent to the pub.

By two o'clock in the afternoon everything and everyone were in place, apart from Nigel and Othman who were making their way to Bethnal Green in Nigel's BMW.

'So how certain are we that the shipment is going to show up?' asked Othman.

'100%. The lorry is being tracked and the last reports show that the vehicle is two miles away from the drop off.'

'Will we get there on time?'

'No problem, one more turning and we'll be there. Get ready for your first London showdown Othman.'

'Can't wait, I'll be watching your back.'

They arrived some 50 yards away from the warehouse ensuring they were out of sight of the pub. The wasteland was full of bushes, abandoned tyres, bottles and general rubbish abandoned by fly tippers who were accustomed to using the area as a dumping ground. In the distance they could see the warehouse. This was made up of derelict skeletal buildings with countless windowless holes and broken walls giving the appearance of a second world war battle scene following the destruction by RAF (or Lufthansa) bombers. Beyond these buildings stood the more elegant structures of the city with the NatWest building dominating the skyline.

Nigel checked that everybody was in place and motioned Othman to get out of the car and make for the nearest bush. They both sat there for a few minutes waiting for the lead officer to notify them of the approach of the lorry. They waited. Nothing happened. It should be here by now, thought Nigel, thinking that the dealers may have sussed them out. He crouched behind the bush next to Othman and felt his bowels loosen. Oh no, he was going to let rip – those damned vodkas! But no, the moment past, he was in control again.

'Where are they?' asked Othman.

'I don't know. Just hold on.'

And as he said those words, a big green lorry appeared on the scene, making towards the warehouse.

'This is it' proclaimed Nigel as he rushed towards the next bush which was located about twenty yards from the entrance of the warehouse. 'Keep your head down and follow me.'

Othman obeyed as they stealthily moved nearer to where the lorry had parked.

'Hold on. Wait for the signal.'

The doors of the warehouse were suddenly opened and the lorry moved towards the entrance. At the same time four armed officers suddenly appeared from nowhere and ran towards the entrance instructing the driver to stop. Instead the lorry accelerated and passed the doors within a matter of seconds. But the vehicle was too slow. The officers ran past the lorry and bid the driver to slow down brandishing their firearms as they did so. At the same time the dealers, who'd been hiding in the warehouse, burst on to the scene, coming from every 'nook and cranny' within the shambles of the building's interior. They were all holding weapons of some description.

'Hold still and put your firearms down' shouted the officers.

The dealers hesitated, looked at each other and decided to comply. The officers kept shouting ordering them to kneel down and put their hands on their heads. There were three dealers; one looked like a Kazakhstan wrestler – bald with no neck; the other two were comparatively thin, wearing sun glasses, sporting beards and looking decidedly shady. The lead officer dragged the driver out of his cab and ordered him to open the back of the lorry. This he did without question as he knew the game was up and didn't fancy a tangle with four armed officers who were itching to assert their authority by way of exercising their weapons.

At that point Nigel and Othman turned up with Nigel ordering the driver to uncover the load which was stored in the back of the lorry. There was furniture, beds, kitchen sinks and other domestic items hiding the main hoard which was stashed at the back end of the lorry. Nigel jumped on to the vehicle and made for the hoard which was covered with brown paper. He took his knife and began tearing away at the paper and string until he found a number of cupboard boxes. He opened one of them and found polythene bags of white powder. He cut one of them open and smelt the contents – pure 100% cocaine.

'Okay you guys. You're all arrested on suspicion of dealing with an illegal drug. You may...'

'Cut the crap officer, we know what you're saying so just get on with it' said the gang member with no neck who was obviously not from Kazakhstan – in fact, he had quite a posh accent with a hint of Irish thrown in for good measure.

'Okay, just stay where you're are. What's your name tiger?' pointing to the Irishman.

'Tony Blair' said Grant O'Malley who'd taken a day's compassionate leave on the pretence that his brother-in- law had passed away the previous day.

'Okay paddy and the rest of you. Get into the vans outside and we'll take you to the local nick. Othman get in touch with HQ and tell them to get the drugs squad down here. They're going to be pissed off big time for this one.'

'Why?'

'Because we've just made them redundant – us doing their job 'an all' (Nigel put on a southern states accent) – they're going to tell us to concentrate on what we're paid to do.'

'And what's that?'

'Anything which doesn't involve drugs... now, let's get a move on.'

At the station the three dealers were questioned and swore blind they didn't know who the supplier was. Nigel advised them their rights and told them, effectively, that they'd be let off if they named their sources. They declined preferring to take their chances in court knowing that after sentencing they would be free within three months ready to start afresh with their lucrative drug dealing set up. The system couldn't cope and, if truth be known, the people involved in the system couldn't cope – it was all out of control.

Having said all that, Grant O'Malley was in control and made a quick phone call to Luke advising him that he needed to pay up or suffer the consequences. Luke owed him about 20k and he needed that money now – to get him released on bail and a return to his trader's job. He couldn't rely on the brother-in-law routine any longer and looked forward to a return to 9 to 5 work.

On receiving this message Luke had, what he thought, was a panic attack. He'd heard about such attacks on LBC radio so knew something of their nature – difficulty in breathing, a fear of experiencing a heart attack and a feeling, as a consequence, of utter panic.

'I'll get it to you as soon as possible Grant.'

'Not good enough. This has been going on for too long. You owe me Luke and I need the cash now.

Transfer the money to my account tomorrow or I'll get one of my colleagues, of which there are many, to cut your damned throat. Do you understand?'

'Understood.'

'Good.'

Luke didn't transfer the money and Grant, expecting jail, ended up on a suspended sentence due firstly to him disclosing the details of his supplier (such grassing up wouldn't serve him well but he was now a desperate man), and, secondly, to some technicality his lawyer had referred to at the beginning of proceedings. But the story didn't end there. As Grant said, he had many friends and wasn't about to forget Luke's debt.

CHAPTER FOUR

Natalie Barham was dismayed to find a mouse mask in the post. She was not a mouse – far from it – she was a civil service tigress, at least, that's the way she viewed herself. When she read the email from Jess it reminded her of times past bringing back memories both good and bad.

Natalie came from a poor family who'd struggled on a council estate in South London. However, she was the brightest of her three siblings and excelled at school at an early stage. She spent hours on the top bunk reading her books. Unlike most of her friends she knew exactly where she was in relation to the world map. She knew that Morden was south of Wimbledon while Stevenage was north of London.

She even knew where Japan and Indonesia could be located on the globe. She had a fascination with places, the countryside, seas, rocks and rivers and so, eventually, got a first class degree in geography and became a fast-tracked civil servant.

Natalie never married although she'd had her fair share of boyfriends. At uni she was sought after on a regular basis which rattled Jess who, at every opportunity in the flat, insinuated, in a fun-loving way, that Nat was the 'souf Landon ore' who couldn't resist anything in trousers. The banter between them was friendly on the surface and they got on for the sake of flat harmony – but there were undertones of contempt. Jess never quite came to terms with the fact that Nat had made good despite her council estate background, while Nat loathed Jess because she was a posh arrogant snob. Of course, these accusations never reared their heads in a spiteful way – although so it seemed – and the two of them co-existed as friendly rivals. They ate together, got drunk together, joked with each other and, when it came to party time, stuck together.

Natalie worked at the Ministry of Defence and had progressed to the senior grades. She owned an elegant two bedroom flat in Battersea and could be seen during the summer months running up and down the Thames Embankment as part of her very disciplined fitness programme.

Before she joined the Civil Service she went travelling with Julia Smith, her uni flat mate, and the two of them spent six months in Australia, earning money working on a farm, followed by six months in India undertaking charity work in an orphanage in Delhi. Natalie and Julia came from similar backgrounds. They had a good work ethic instilled in them at an early age by parents who were by no means rich but maintained high standards of behaviour and integrity. They were also caring, again influenced by their parents who had stuck together through thick and thin in order to preserve the stability of their respective families.

On returning from their travels Natalie joined the Civil Service while Julia went back to college to gain her PGCE so that she could become a fully qualified primary school teacher. She obtained her qualifications and went on to teach in a primary school in Tooting.

Consequently the two had kept in touch and became lifelong friends. Julia got married when she was 28 and now had two children aged three and five. Natalie on the other hand had no desire to marry and following a string of boyfriends decided to concentrate on her career to see how far she could get up the ladder. She proved to be a very effective manager and ruled with an iron fist. Nevertheless she was fair and considerate with her staff – congratulated them when they'd done well, reprimanded them when they fell short.

It was while she was running on a sunny Saturday morning in July that she got the call. she stopped by a park bench and took her mobile from her pocket:

'Hi Nat, Julia. Can you talk?'

'Hi Julia, just doing a bit of running but great to hear from you.'

'I can phone back?'

'No, no. I need a rest. Let me sit down and sort myself out and I'll be with you.'

Natalie sat herself down, took a drink from her bottle, wiped her face and said:

'How's it going Julia?'

'Everything's fine. No problems but have you checked your emails?'

'Not today.'

'Well I've just heard from Jess, our uni flat mate. Do you remember her?'

'Remember her. How could anyone forget Jess – pompous bitch.'

'Now, now Nat, she weren't that bad.'

'I know, I know. We had a love hate relationship. Anyway, what about her?'

'She 's invited me to a dinner party, a sort of uni reunion in August.'

'Are you going?'

'Why not. But that's not the end of it.'

'What do you mean?'

'She sent me a cat's mask which I've got to wear. The idea is that we don't know who's who until we reveal ourselves.'

'Yeah, I've got the same message. She's given me a mouse mask, the bitch.'

'But I thought you didn't know about this?'

'I played dumb to see if you were up for it or not. If you weren't going, I wasn't going.'

'Well, let's go together. The crazy thing is that she's told everybody what mask they should be wearing and hasn't thought through the possibility that we're all in touch so we'll know what masks we're wearing.'

'That will make it even more hilarious because we'll make out we don't know each other, and put on weird accents, but at the same time we'll know exactly who we are.'

'Well you and I will know each other. But there may be others there who are not in contact and will be totally unknown until they reveal themselves.'

'True, but who else would she invite?'

'Probably Nigel Francis and Othman.'

'Oh yes. I'd forgotten about them. Do you keep in touch?'

'No. Haven't seen or heard from them since uni.'

'I wonder what they're up to? I quite fancied Othman.'

'I think they became policemen. Something like that. Anyway are we going or not?'

'I'm up for it if you are Julia. Jess probably wants to use this as an opportunity to show off her mansion but it will give us a chance to politely take the piss.'

'She may not have a mansion. She may be poor like us.'

'I doubt it – she'll have a big house, big car, subservient husband and a massive ego, mark my words.'

'Well, in fairness if she's polite and welcoming, I'm not going to drag up old sores. I wouldn't want to destroy her party for no good reason.'

'True and nor would I. But if Jess starts misbehaving, the rules on etiquette round the dinner table will have to be temporarily abandoned. I never took any shit from Jess at uni and I don't intend taking any now, especially as we're all supposed to be grown up.'

'Go girl. This will be an interesting night.'

CHAPTER FIVE

The following week Jess arranged to see her Wednesday coffee set but as it was raining and her hair had just been dyed, she didn't want to risk exposing her head to the bad weather. She'd thought about wearing a hat, and even contemplated using an umbrella, but, after due consideration, had decided such protection would've proved inadequate, especially as high winds had been forecast earlier that morning. There was no way she was going to have her hair ruined having spent a fortune on having it trimmed and coloured. No, the ladies would have to come to her house. Besides, her house was the largest and offered kitchen diner facilities in a room which measured thirty – five by seventeen feet. This, of course did not include the ten foot square utility room and was additional to the main dining room which measured thirty by twenty feet. Jess loved to refer to footage when describing her property – again it all went back to precision and attention to detail. This made her unique, as far as she was concerned, in the neighbourhood. She was always spouting on about size and proportion, and the measurements of her rooms offered another opportunity to impress those who needed impressing. The kitchen diner was perfect; it offered quality cutlery, crockery and furnishings and was more than suitable for the Wednesday ladies who, on one hand, were not related to royalty, but on the other, were respectable figures in the local community (despite Joy's reputation as a bi-sexual cougar !).

She'd spent most of the morning cleaning the kitchen after her children had finished their breakfasts and, having reluctantly got dressed in their green uniforms, had left the house under the strict supervision of Olga who was tasked with transporting them to school in the newly purchased Range Rover. It was a typical morning apart from the fact that the ladies were going to meet at her home for morning coffee, and cakes she'd prepared the previous day. She knew they would be impressed with her house but wanted to impress them more – this time to reveal how witty and daring she could be. After polishing the tiled floor for the third time she made her way to her bedroom and pulled out a box that was lying on the top shelf of one of her fitted wardrobes. It was a white circular box measuring about two feet across and one foot in depth. She laid it on her bed and opened the lid. After removing the crate paper she saw her beautiful swan outfit. This consisted of an ordinary but extravagant mask decorated in silver and blue sequins and a white skull cap, which obviously went over her head. This cap supported a long S shaped white neck which led to a beautiful swan's head equipped with eyes, nostrils and a beautiful orangey yellowy beak. The base of the neck had been carefully sewn to the top of the skull cap and was strengthened with wire so that it wouldn't droop. Beneath this swan outfit were some large feathery wings which could be unfolded and attached to a white leotard by a series of hooks and fasteners. To complete the picture a white tutu, white tights and white ballet shoes were lifted from the bottom of the box and displayed on the bed alongside the other regalia, the site of which made Jess jubilant. 'Today Matthew I'm going to be a swan' she screamed as she flung her dressing gown across the room revealing a slim, shapely naked body (apart from her g string which left little to the imagination).

Jess discarded the ballet shoes preferring to wear her white high heels and gazed at herself in her full attire in the giant mirror which covered one end of the room for at least 15 minutes. She was a picture of whiteness with a swan's neck and head coming out from the top of her own. 'I am a swan' she cried.

⇌ ⇌

About an hour later the three ladies rang the door bell. Jess opened the door and went into a swan like pose. There was an initial silence as the ladies tried to fathom out exactly what had answered the door. To say they were in a state of shock would be an understatement. Joy, the brightest of the three, remembered something about wearing masks at a reunion and the penny dropped:

'Oh it's you Jess. You've got a wobbly white thing on your head.'

'It's a swan's head Joy. I'm a swan.'

'Ah yes now I see' said Martha. 'You *are* a swan.'

'It's for my reunion. What do you think?'

'It's different Jess' said June, trying not to laugh.

'Different? It's a work of art. It's me, don't you see? I'm slim and graceful like a swan and now I'm disguised as a swan. In fact it makes me feel like a swan. In fact I believe I *am* a swan. It's a perfect match. The others are going to be so impressed.'

'What others?' Martha asked.

'You know my uni reunion – what we were talking about last week. Anyway, come in. I want to show you my new kitchen diner furniture.'

Jess waddled into her kitchen and as she did so the swan's neck wobbled in unison. She looked ridiculous although none of them had the nerve to say so. There was a small three piece suite in the corner of the room and they decided to use this furniture rather than the kitchen dining table.

'Is this the new furniture Jess?'

'Yes. What do you think?'

'It's lovely. Where did you get it?'

'Where do you think?'

'Harrods?'

'Where else darling.'

'Thought so. Bet it cost a bomb.'

'Not really. The sofa was in a sale and I managed to negotiate a lower price for the two armchairs.'

'How much in all?'

'About 10K. Not bad eh?'

They all looked at each other and slyly raised their eye brows. '*Oh my God*' they all thought. '*Ten thousand for a three piece suite? We could never justify that sort of money on what looked like a very average piece of furniture.*' These were the thoughts buzzing through their heads.

'Great value' piped up Joy. 'Looking for some decent furniture myself – now I know where to look.'

'Harrods?' asked Jess.

'No. The second hand furniture store on Tooting High Street. There's no way I'd pay 10k for a three piece suite.'

'Suit yourself darling, but if you want quality, you have to pay for it' Jess said as she approached one of the armchairs.

At first she had difficulty in sitting down as her wings flapped open every time she took position. However, after folding her wings properly using the adjustment provided, she was able to sit more comfortably.

'Right' she said 'coffee for everyone?'

'Yes please' they all chanted.

'What's a baby swan called Jess?' asked Joy.

'I think it's called a cygnet.'

'Right, That's it. We are your cygnets Jess. You are the mother swan and we are your babies.'

'Are you taking the piss Joy? I'm not really a swan, I'm just pretending.'

'Sorry Jess we are taking the piss a bit. Although your costume is great, you do look a bit weird when you move around – the swan's neck wobbles a lot.'

'I know that June. Don't you see, it's all part of my humour. I know I look a complete pratt but that's all part of it. You don't think I'm taking this seriously do you?'

'Well, we did a bit Jess – at the beginning anyway' said Martha.

'Well relax. Now let me make the coffee.'

Jess tried to get up from her armchair but her wings became entangled and she failed to gain sufficient momentum to propel herself forward. Her friends came to her rescue and pulled her off the armchair.

'Sod this outfit girls' she said kicking off her high heels and unclipping her wings 'But what do you think? Will it create a bit of a hoot when my uni mates come round?'

'Of course it will' they all responded in unison as Jess took off her mask and skull cap 'you're going to be a star.'

Jess busied herself with the coffees and cakes while the others discussed the weather.

'Shall I bring some biscuits over?' she asked.

'Why not' June said 'Let's have a carbo feast.'

They sat round the coffee table discussing the usual – sex, makeup and shopping et cetera and then the conversation returned to the reunion in August.

'I would love to be a fly on the wall' said June. 'You with your swan's outfit, the others dressed as cats, dogs and slugs or whatever. I'd love to be there. Wouldn't you girls?'

'Too right said Joy but it is a uni reunion and Jess needs to respect that.'

'Well there won't be too many there and there's always the chance it will be an utter flop. You just don't know how people have changed. We might end up arguing and worse. We all got on okay because we were all in the same boat. But there were one or two fall outs. I don't want our reunion turning into one bloody big row,'

'I'm sure it won't Jess' said June. 'All I was saying was that I'd love to see you lot together – observe from afar if you know what I mean.'

'Yes I get that.' Jess paused as she turned things over in her mind. 'Wait a minute. The whole point of this really is to masquerade so that no one knows who anybody is. It doesn't have to be a full blown reunion. That would be an important part, of course. But I see no reason why you guys can't come – disguised of course. That would bolster up the numbers and, if it all goes pear shaped, I'll have you three to support me. What do you think?'

'Great idea' said June.

'I want to be a gorilla' said Martha.

'No Martha that mask has already been allocated. How about a sloth?'

'What's that?'

'A slow, lazy, sleepy, furry loveable creature – perfect for you Martha.'

'I'm not too sure whether that's a compliment or not. I'll google when I get home.'

'Take it as a compliment, I've got some claws you can wear as well... now getting back to logistics, I think I'll have to restrict it to you guys and my four flat mates. That will make a total of eight. No partners. I can mange eight. I don't need to tell my uni friends that you're coming. They'll just think you're other uni friends. By the time we all take our masks off we'll all be pissed in any case. Besides I can say you went to the same uni but in a different year. We knew each other then and reacquainted ourselves in Wimbledon. It doesn't matter whether I'm making it up or not. In any case it will be a hoot. Perhaps you can help me prepare?'

'I can make a cake' June said.

'I'll provide some bubbly' said Martha.

'I'll bring my whip just in case anybody fancies a bit of domination' said Joy.

'That's great but I would really appreciate you getting here say one hour before the party starts so you can give me some help with the preparation. I'll be nervous on the day, believe it or not, and I'll need a bit of moral support.'

'It's a done deal Jess.'

CHAPTER SIX

Grant O'Malley managed to cling on to his job and decided to keep a low profile as far as drug dealing was concerned. Thankfully he didn't owe anybody anything and, apart from the Luke problem, was able to concentrate on his legitimate trading. His relationship with Luke was strained to say the least and their partnership was all but finished. Luke made every attempt to avoid him and there was certainly no socialising in the pub. No, the situation was tense and an awkward atmosphere could be felt in the offices. The fact of the matter was, at the end of the day, Luke owed him 20k and that had to be paid up. Luke, on the other hand, was struggling. He had no more drugs to sell and his trading performance was deteriorating. This decline in performance was probably due to a mixture of fear and bad luck.

One lunchtime when the market activity appeared to subside, Luke decided to take a break and made his way to the coffee machine. He bought himself a coffee and a mars bar and sat himself in the recreational area. Others had the same idea and soon the area was packed with traders. When he finished he went to the loo and started to take a long but satisfying leak. As he was concentrating on his flow and without warning:

'How's it hanging Luke?' Grant asked as he took position in the neighbouring urinal.

Luke was startled and quickly finished what he was doing, shook his equipment, tucked it in his underpants and zipped his trousers – all in one motion.

'Fine Grant, see you later.'

'Not so fast buddy. Let me finish here and we'll talk.'

'No time Grant, got to go.'

Grant grabbed his shoulder with his left hand as he steadied his equipment with his right.

'Not so fast Luke, you owe me.'

'Look Grant, not now. We've both got things to do. I'll speak to you later.'

'That's not good enough. I want to speak now you bastard. I'm not waiting anymore' and without warning Grant pushed Luke to the wall and kneed him in the groin. Luke doubled up in pain. There was no one else in the toilet so Grant took the opportunity to finish the job. He grabbed Luke's ear and twisted it until Luke begged him to stop. As he did so he rose up and punched Grant in the stomach and smacked him on the side of the head. Before Grant could recover Luke made his exit leaving Grant O'Malley dazed and angry.

'There's no point running Luke. I'll get you in the end' he shouted as Luke disappeared down the corridor.

He got up from the floor and looked at himself in the mirror. As he did so another trader appeared on the scene and asked him if everything was okay.

'You look a bit shaken mate, do you want me to get some help?'

'No, no don't bother. Had a bit of a turn and cracked my head. Nothing to worry about. It's these pain killers I'm on. They've got horrendous side effects. I'll be alright thanks.'

'Okay, I can call first aid if you want?'

'No, don't bother. I'll be alright in a few minutes.'

The trader took a leak, washed his hands, had one more look at Grant and then made his exit. Grant watched him as he disappeared down the corridor. He then took his mobile out of his pocket and dialled a number.

'Jon is that you?'

'Yeah, who's this?'

'Grant, Grant O'Malley.'

'How can I help my friend?'

'Got a job for you Jon.'

'What kind of job?'

'One that you'll be good at. I want you to rough up someone.'

'Why?'

'He owes me 20k and won't pay up.'

'How far do you want us to go?'

'Don't kill him, just hurt him bad.'

'Even if he pays up?'

'Yes, although that is highly unlikely. He won't have the cash on him so I'll leave it to you to sort out. If he eventually coughs up, then 5k is yours. You'll probably have to meet him twice.'

'Details?'

'His name is Luke and works as a trader with me. He's tall, good looking and can handle himself. He lives in South West London and uses Raynes Park station.'

'You'll have to be more specific than that.'

'Okay, okay. The best thing to do is for you to meet me at Raynes Park. I'll track him and point him out when we leave the station. You can do the rest.'

'Got it. When.'

'I'll let you know.'

'Expenses?'

'What do you mean?'

'I need some money upfront to deal with my expenses. I'm not waiting until the job's finished- I want some money now – a non refundable deposit if you like.'

'Okay, give me your account details and I'll transfer £500 straightaway. You'll get the rest after the job's complete.'

'Say if he never pays up?'

'Then kill the bastard.'

'You're joking?'

'Yes, of course I am – just hurt him if you know what I mean.'

'No problem – look forward to it.'

CHAPTER SEVEN

It was the morning of the 5th August 2005 and Jess was preparing for her dinner party. They would start with pre dinner drinks with caviar, oysters and other delicacies. This would be washed down with lashings of champagne. She had plenty of beer, spirits, wine and Pimms in reserve just in case anyone didn't like the bubbly stuff. The first course would consist of home- made mushroom or Thai chicken soup followed by a choice comprising either pigeon, salmon or mixed vegetable risotto. The main course would be either venison, lemon sole, chicken or mixed bean salad with baby potatoes, and the dessert would consist of either mixed fruit with crème fraiche or crème caramel or lemon cheesecake. This would be followed with cheese and biscuits. There would be the very best white and red wines from South Africa and sweet wines from France. Port, whisky and brandy would be served with the cheese and biscuits (as well as wine).

On the same day Joy was concentrating on her abs having completed her first training session of the day. She now had a one hour break before her next client and was intent on giving her stomach a good work out. She wanted to look good for this evening's dinner party and if that meant strenuous exercise followed by a session on the sun bed, then so be it. She would be on the prowl tonight, especially as she would be wearing a tiger's mask, and hoped there would be single attractive people about. On the other hand, who cared about whether they were single or not – she would be on the prowl in any case. 'Grrrrrr' she roared!

Martha had taken her kids to school and had returned to her two bed roomed terraced house in South Wimbledon. Her plan that morning was to attend her weekly yoga lesson, visit her parents and then join the communal chant at the local Buddhist temple. She was both Buddhist and Christian – two religions were better than one for insurance purposes! She would then return home, have a shower, try her sloth mask on, get dressed, take her sloth mask off and make her way to Jess's house to help with the preparations. In between all this she would try to find time to collect the kids or, if time ran out, get her mother to pick them up.

June was particularly excited as she was the one who showed most interest in the reunion, stating that she would love to be a fly on the wall during the proceedings. She had been given a Frankenstein mask which Luke had jokingly told her to keep on as it would scare her students if she took it off, and, ignoring his poor attempt at humour, had stored it in her suitcase ready for collection after she had lectured on the anatomy of the duck billed platypus at Kingston University for two periods in the afternoon. After this she would make her way to Jessica's house to help with preparations. Jess wanted her to stay the night and June was more than happy to do this.

Nigel had earned himself a few brownie points with the recent capture of drug dealers in Bethnal Green and had kept off the booze for at least a week. He'd put his wolf mask on a number of times and felt the whole idea was a bit stupid. He would play along and hoped that after a couple of drinks he'd be able to get into the swing of the party. He pondered on his short relationship with Jessica. She had been (and probably still was) an attractive blond with a big mouth. Her sexiness oozed wherever she went but once she started talking, the appeal subsided. That's what he found in any case. He remembered the two of them going for a cheap pub meal in their uni days. They hadn't much money but could afford chicken and chips and a couple of pints. Anyway, things were going well until he mentioned the Afghan war. He told her he was dead against the Soviet invasion and was angered by the West's apathy. He can remember the conversation as if it were yesterday:

'We should have done something to stop that war. The Soviets had no right to invade.'

'Nonsense' Jess replied. 'They were invited to invade to crush the rebels. The Soviets wanted to prop up the communist government to ward off the Mujahideen.'

'The Mujahideen? Who are they?'

'You don't know your history do you Nigel. The Mujahideen were insurgent groups who wished to topple the Afghan government.'

'I didn't know you were a communist Jess?'

'I'm not you idiot, but nor do I believe in rebellions. You can't have groups of people holding a government to ransom using violence to demonstrate their case.'

'But they probably didn't want to be suppressed or treated unfairly - no one does.'

'That's bullshit. You have to respect your government no matter who's in charge.'

'That's also bullshit Jess. Besides look what happened when they did invade – thousands of innocent people died. What was the point?'

'That's the price of war. A government can't stand by and let a load of rebels take over.'

'Depends on the cause. If the government was corrupt then someone had to revolt.'

'Well, whatever way you look at it, it was inevitable that there was going to be fighting.'

'Like most wars, it was utterly pointless' he said. 'Look what happened when the Soviets withdrew. The rebels couldn't get their act together and the country ended up in civil war... utter madness. More innocent people died as a consequence. The Soviets shouldn't have got involved in the first place.'

'They had to. Innocent People were dying before they invaded. It's war – people die.'

'You sound a bit callous Jess.'

'And you sound a bit of a wimp Nigel. When the going gets tough I want a man who can make decisions.'

'Fine, as long as they are the right ones.'

'But sometimes you just don't know. You have to follow your instincts.'

'So you wouldn't mind pressing the nuclear button on the basis of your instinct?'

'No I wouldn't and nor should you. My God, you're a sportsman and a bit of a hunk. I thought you had guts?'

'I like to think I do, but I also weigh up the pros and cons before making any important decision.'

'Don't we all? But you're coming over as one of those people who gets caught up with the analysis of the problem and fails to make any clear decision – analysis paralysis – I think they call it.'

'And you, my dear Jess are coming over as a bit of a war monger – hungry for blood.'

'Well maybe I am. The Middle East needed and still needs a good kicking to get it into shape.'

'You are joking?'

'No I'm not'.

Jess's countenance had changed as if she were suffering from some sort of schizophrenia. Either that or she was completely pissed. She gazed into space for a split second and then blurted:

'It's lily livered people like you who are letting the side down.'

Nigel recoiled, he hadn't seen this side of Jess before – he didn't like it.

'Oh really, well this lily livered person is ready to go. Let's agree to disagree, go back to the flat, get our clothes off and do what we do best.'

'I don't make love to cowards so you can forget about that.'

'Are you for real? You've gone completely mad and unreasonable. Either that or you're just having a laugh.'

'I'm not mad and I'm not having a laugh. These are serious issues.'

'I know that but you're not making any sense.'

'Well, I think I am.'

'Well fine. Do you want to go now or not?'

'No I don't. But if you want to go, go – we have completely different views on things like this.'

With that Nigel left her in the pub. She was right – they were clearly different people with opposing views. Jess had also, without warning, changed into an aggressive opinionated bitch - she was definitely not for him. In any case, her arguments were completely irrational and totally flawed - as far as he was concerned. Anyway, after that little discussion their relationship was never the same and although they co existed in the flat, there was always a tension between the two of them. It will be interesting tonight when he turns up as a wolf – ready to pounce and devour – and prove perhaps that he is not so *lily- livered*!

Othman went about his duties in the normal way but was now itching to have a case he could get his teeth into. He had shadowed his friend, Nigel, for a number of months and was ready to lead a case of his own on behalf of the Met. For many years he'd been accustomed to serving in Cairo and solving crimes in the backstreets of this sprawling city. However, London was different – more rules and regulations, more diversity, more gangs, more drugs and more civil crime. He'd now made the transition and felt he'd adapted well to his new circumstances. He knew what the UK was like as he'd attended university there, so from that perspective, had an insight into the many cultures that operated within different communities up and down the country.

He'd bought himself a one bedroom flat in Putney and had made friends with a crowd connected to the Fulham Football Club. These guys usually met up in the *Spotted Horse* on a Wednesday night and if Othman wasn't on shift he'd have a couple of pints with them. He tried to attend most of the home games and felt comfortable in their presence at these events. In the main, his group consisted of professionals – lawyers, accountants, builders and business owners. They were not your typical football hooligan type – far from it, and analysed each game applying an intellect and narrative that would have been admired by the likes of Sir Trevor Brooking or Gary Lineker. Othman became a respected figure within the Fulham football fraternity and although his friends knew he was a copper, this did not hamper the relationship in any way or form.

It was on one Wednesday night that he met Lucy Deekin, an avid Fulham supporter and local police officer. They met by chance. He was ordering his second pint of Youngs when he accidentally knocked into her at the bar. They struck up a conversation and the rest is history. Lucy was a South London girl from a poor family living in Roehampton. She did well at school, went to Hendon Training College, qualified as an officer, married another copper, got divorced and was now living the life she wanted in South West London. She was not looking for anybody when she bumped into Othman but after a couple of dates realised that this man ticked all the right boxes – he was kind, witty, clever and good looking. What's more she felt comfortable with him. She was never bored when he was around and looked forward to his calls. She may, in fact, be falling for him in a big way – although it was too early to let these feelings be known to him. As for Othman, he found Lucy attractive, bubbly, intelligent and entertaining. He didn't know whether he was ready to settle down so he, like her, was playing it cool. They both decided to let the relationship grow, without any pressure, and see where the mood would take them.

I t was on the morning of the dinner party that Lucy decided to pop round to Othman's flat on the off chance he might be around. She would normally phone him first but thought she would arrive unannounced just to see his reaction. In any case, she was on the late shift and wanted to do a bit of shopping in Putney High Street - this would be her excuse for popping in.

'Hi Lucy. This is a surprise. Great to see you. Come in.'

'I hope it's convenient' she said, taking off her coat as she walked past the front door. 'I've got to do a bit of shopping this morning so I thought I'd pop in for a quick chat about tomorrow night.'

'Don't tell me, you can't make it?'

'I'm afraid not. Just had my shift altered. I'm on lates from tomorrow. I could make tonight if you're around?'

'Ah, what a shame. Come in and sit down and I'll tell you all about it.'

Othman's main room was tastefully decorated. It had expensive looking polished floorboards with Persian rugs placed opposite the iron fireplace and under the bay window. The windows were original with sash cords hanging alongside the frames which could be used to lift and lower the window panes. They looked in excellent condition. Around the rugs were placed two small sofas which could accommodate no more than two people each. They were made from a thick material stained dark blue with a Japanese floral design printed on the surface. A coffee table with a tiled surface supported a silver coffee set and a silver Buddha which must have been eight inches high. At the back of the room was a small antique (regency) table with four chairs of similar design tucked neatly away so they wouldn't take up too much space in what could only be described as a relatively small dining area.

Some tasteful pictures hung on the freshly painted white walls together with various photos of friends and relatives. Overall the room generated a modern but friendly atmosphere with touches of tradition and, indeed, antiquity which provided a certain charm to the whole ambience of the place.

'This is lovely' said Lucy as she sat down on one of the sofas. 'Did you decorate the room yourself?'

'With the help of a few friends... I chose most of the furniture but a close friend did all the painting.'

'Who's your close friend?'

'Oh, a guy called Nigel. We went to uni together. In fact that's what I wanted to talk about. Do you want tea or coffee first?'

'I'll have coffee... that would be great.'

Othman went out to the kitchen and continued with the conversation:

'You see I've been invited to a uni reunion tonight which I can't really get out of.'

'And nor should you. We can always meet up another time.'

'Yes but I think I would prefer to go out with you then meet up with some of my old flat mates – especially as we've got to wear masks.'

'What?'

'Yeah, the girl who's running it – a bit of a screw ball – wants us to be in disguise so we don't recognise anyone.'

'A bit weird but I suppose it'll be a laugh once everybody has had a few drinks. What are you going as Oth?'

'A gorilla.'

'Brilliant. Let me see you your costume.'

'It's not a costume, just a mask. The whole thing's stupid as some of us have worked out who's going and what they'll be wearing. We'll just play along with the game so as not to upset the hostess.'

'You'll have a great time – now let me see you in your gorilla mask. You never know, it might turn me on.'

'I doubt it' said Othman as he placed the tray holding the coffees on the coffee table.

＝≷┼ ┼≷＝

Natalie decided to have a lay- in on the day of the party as she'd had the week from hell at the office. Her boss was the classic chauvinist pig who resented her success and used every opportunity to catch her out. He was typically old school and believed the woman's place was in the home – certainly not in the office. On the other hand, he felt insecure and feared that someday she would show him up in front of his colleagues on a question that he should really know the answer to - but didn't - while she was able to answer without hesitation. Such a situation hadn't materialised but he lived in fear that it would. During the last week, he had been trying to find fault in her response to emails in terms of their timeliness but failed miserably and so embarked upon a cutting remark regime which, on one occasion, led to her being on the verge of losing it. Thankfully, she hadn't and, instead, thought of ways she could reap revenge with her remaining unscathed while he was hung out to dry. However, all this scheming wasn't doing anything for her health and by the time the week was over she'd become anxious and exhausted. So she lay in bed thinking about her week from hell. Then she remembered her party and decided to try out her mask. She put her mouse mask on and looked in the mirror – pathetic she thought.

On the other hand Julia delighted in wearing her cat's mask and paraded up and down her hallway eyeing herself in the full length mirror as she did so. Unlike Natalie, she'd had a stress free week at the primary school in which she worked, and had discussed, in great detail, the story of her time at uni with her husband, and retold several times her experiences in the flat where she, and others, had to contend with the massive mood swings of one Jessica Garnett.

So, in summary, everything had been prepared for the great dinner party. Jess would be a swan; Nigel, a wolf; Othman, a gorilla; Natalie, a mouse; Julia, a cat; Martha, a sloth; Joy, a tiger and June a Frankenstein monster – everything was set for an interesting night.

CHAPTER EIGHT

A ndrew, Jess's husband had decided to keep a low profile and, on the morning of the party, had decided to lock himself in his study. He didn't care much for Jess's coffee set and, on the odd occasion she'd disclosed what they'd got up to during their meetings, he'd mentally switched off to avoid having to think about what he'd regarded as meaningless trivia. When he found out about the reunion and the masquerading, he rolled up his eyes in anticipation of an unstoppable, not to mention, embarrassing disaster. There would be drunkenness, shouting and, possibly, food throwing, which he had no intention of being party to. Instead he would play with the kids, put them to bed and then hideaway in his study. Fortunately, the children's bedrooms were located at the other end of the house so they wouldn't have to suffer the inevitable rowdiness which, he calculated, would probably start from around 9 pm and end any time after midnight. No, he would stay in his study and listen to Brahms. At worse, if the noise increased, he would play delightful melodies from the Edgar Broughton Band – a three piece heavy metal trio who'd caused eardrums to perforate in the seventies. Playing this band at high volume should be enough to drown their commotion and, hopefully, drive them back to where they came from.

'Andrew' Jess bellowed from the kitchen.

'Yes my dear?'

'Can you stop playing with the kids for one minute and help us in the kitchen. We need a potato peeler and you're the man for the job.'

'Certainly me dear.'

Andrew ambled into the kitchen and was confronted by three anxious looking women.

'We need some help round here Andrew. This is Martha. Say hello to her.'

'Hello Martha.'

'And this is June.'

'Hello June.'

They both acknowledged him and then went about their delegated duties. Martha, on strict instruction, was to prepare the table and June was to prepare the desserts. Jess was to prepare everything else except the drinks.

'Now Andrew. I want you to prepare the drinks. Please listen to what I have to say. I'm only going to say this once. I want you to bring six bottles of white and six bottles of red from the cellar. That's your first job. Make sure they come from the batch delivered last Sunday. Secondly, I want you to go back to the cellar and collect four bottles of the best bubbly. Bring all this stuff up and put the white wine and bubbly in the fridge. You can leave the reds under the sideboard over there. Are you getting all of this Andrew?'

'Of course my dear. What about spirits and beer?'

'Do I have to explain everything? You know where that's all kept so place the spirits on the sideboard and put the beers in the second fridge.'

'Consider it done o masterful wife.'

'Don't be sarcastic Andrew, it doesn't suit you. And don't forget the glasses. Have them displayed on the other sideboard and place the appropriate wine glasses on the table – Martha will help you if you don't know what glasses go with what drinks. You'll help him won't you Martha.'

'Of course I will. Hello Andrew.'

'Hello again Martha.'

'You'd better go and fetch the wine' she said.

'Yes. I better had.'

'And don't forget the sweet wine' Jess bellowed as he disappeared through the door way of the cellar. 'And don't forget to clean the glasses' she screamed... 'and Andrew?'

'Yes?'

'Don't forget the lagers – some people prefer lager to bitter so don't forget them.'

'Of course not my dear' he whispered to himself as he clutched the banister leading down to the basement – 'I'd like to drown you in them' he said in a louder voice as he collected the first bottle of white from the wine rack. He could say what he wanted down in the basement because his beloved wife couldn't hear him.

On completion of this assignment he was given potatoes, carrots and leeks to peel. He did this without interruption from Jess and was able to slip away back to the kids in the playroom. A few minutes later:

'Where's Andrew?' Jess asked.

'Don't know' Martha and June said in unison. 'Do we need him for anything else?'

'I suppose not, but I like to have him near at hand just in case there's anything I want him to do...Andrew' she shouted 'where in God's name are you?'

Andrew's head popped out from around the corner:

'I'm free' he said in a John Inman voice.

'Well come over here Andrew, I've got something else for you to do. And don't speak like that. You're not funny even though Martha and June are laughing. They're laughing out of sympathy, not because they think you're funny.'

'Of course not – you're right, that was a poor attempt at humour. I curse myself for it. I'm sorry my dear. What can I do for you?'

'Promise me that you won't show your face at the dinner party. You know how much I've been looking forward to this and I don't want you ruining everything. Do you understand?'.

Martha and June looked at each other – how could she speak to her husband like this?

'Of course I do. I made it clear from the start that this was your do and that I would keep in the background. I fully intend doing this and I promise I will not do anything to upset your little party.'

'It's not a little party. It's an important party. I will be meeting friends I haven't seen for years and I don't won't any sarcastic remarks from you.'

'I understand. I will keep well out of your way. But if you should need me for anything, please give me a call. I'll be in my study concentrating on the soothing delights of Brahms.'

'Who's Brahms?' Martha asked.

Andrew looked at Martha in a sympathetic way.

'Have you not heard of the expression 'Brahms and Liszt?'

'No.'

'It's cockney rhyming slang for getting pissed.'

'Oh I see, I thought it might have something to do with music?'

'Not tonight my dear Martha, not tonight.'

CHAPTER NINE

The wolf and gorilla arrived together and were welcomed by the swan.

'Hello wolf
hello gorilla
I'm a swan as you can see
do come in for a cup of tea.'

Nigel and Othman looked at each other with joint realisation that it was Jess (obviously) and that she was going to use poetic verse to communicate. 'Oh God' they both thought.

Wolf and gorilla both mumbled thanks and made their way to the dining room. Swan followed with a tray supporting glasses of champagne.

'Please try my champagne
you two beasts
and surrender to the grape
Take your time
drink it slow
while I bring out the cake'.

With that Jess disappeared.

Nigel and Othman looked at each other and burst into laughter. Should they play along or tell her the game was up – they decided to play along. Jess returned with a tray of goodies from nuts to things on toasted fingers.

Nigel couldn't resist:

'O swan o swan I do declare
your feathers are so white
Your long slim neck and gorgeous butt
encourages wolves to bite.'

Jess replied:

'O big bad wolf
you must not bite
cos we must have some fun
Drink your wine and socialise
as others are to come.'

With that the door bell rang. Jess opened the door. It was the cat and mouse.

'Oh do come in sweet cat and mouse
and meet the other beasts
Please don't fight but hold a truce
on this fine night at least.'

Natalie and Julia were too shocked to say anything.
Instead they giggled and followed Jess to the dining
room where, on seeing wolf and gorilla, couldn't
hold back their feelings any longer:
    'What the f..k ... this is mad' proclaimed Nat, and
before anybody could say anything else...

'Please don't swear my little mouse
But take a glass of bubbly
You too cat I've got no milk
so try instead to be cuddly.'

Julia got into the mood:

'Oh thank you swan
but what a wobbly neck
how will you eat your food?
I'll drink my wine and chase the mouse
– what else is there to do?'

Nat piped up:

'Don't chase me cat for as you know
I'm filled with poisonous pellets

One bite of me and then you'll see
I'm no tastier than a ferret.'

By this time the four of them were howling with laughter and it was clear that everybody knew who the other was. However, without saying a word, they all knew it would be good fun to keep up the pretence. And so the poetry continued:

'Now that we're here
I think you'll agree
that animals can get on
Just as well, cos as I speak
I feel an itchiness in my thong.'

'That's just plain nonsense' Othman said 'swans don't wear thongs.'

'This one does you... big gorilla.' Jess responded as the door bell rang again.

Swan opened the door and was immediately sprang upon by a tiger. 'Oh my God' she screamed as the tiger tried to bite her neck while pawing at her thighs.

'Stop stop big tiger
you are so rough
please cease your groping now
For if you don't I'll tell the police
to rip away your tail.'

'What an earth are you talking about Jess' asked Joy 'you're talking in riddles.'

'Shhh Joy. You don't know me remember? I'm talking in poetic verse to make the night even more interesting. If you speak try to speak in verse.'

'What do you mean?'

'You know, make the last word rhyme with something you've said before.'

'What a load of bollocks. I can't do that – now where's the bubbly?'

'Follow me, but don't give away who you are and join in the party spirit.'

'I'll try but I'm no William Shakespeare.'

As tiger and swan entered the room sloth and Frankenstein's monster came marching in. Jess offered them champagne which they gulped down straightaway, and then offered the whole party a second glass – and then a third. She then made an announcement:

'O welcome all you beasts of prey
well some of you at least
There's drink and food
and other delights
o joyous is the feast
There's wolf and sloth with cat and mouse
gorilla with a swan
There's tiger too and Frankenstein

let's hope we'll be on song
For beneath it all
these are my friends
from uni and the past
Let's drink another and then we'll discover
Who the f..k we are!'

With that *The Carnival of the Animals* took instruction from Jess regarding the seating arrangements. She had decided to jumble them up so a uni mate would be sitting next to a coffee set mate - as far as reasonably possible. So the table set up looked like this:

Martha	Jess
Othman	Julia
Jo	Nigel
Natalie	June

Meanwhile Andrew, who had secretly sabotaged the desserts with sodium chloride after having got through two bottles of red wine during the course of the day, took position outside the door leading to the hall. The other door led to the kitchen diner so there was no point in him standing there. He was adamant that he was not going to miss this party even though he originally thought it best to stay out the way. No, that wouldn't be right. He wanted Jess to know that he wasn't a walkover. He knew about her affair with

Luke and thought this would be a good time to reveal everything. This, of course, would cause angst and horror for the dinner guests, but he'd had enough. He wanted revenge. Of course, the beauty of doing it this way was that he could ruin Jess's precious dinner party and thereby prove that nothing in life is structured, ordered or, indeed, predictable. So the final set up looked like this:

                    Andrew
              _____ door leading to hallway
    Martha   Jess
    Othman   Julia
    Jo   Nigel
    Natalie   June
            _____ door leading to Kitchen/diner

The masked visitors sat down in their designated places and Jess rang her little bell which was positioned by her knife and fork. In scurried Olga who was wearing a mask and a sexy maid's outfit.

'This is Olga everybody – she will be waiting on us tonight with a little help from me if things get busy. Olga is from Germany and...'

'Austria' Olga interrupted.

'Oh, sorry Olga. Olga is from Austria everybody and she's over here looking after my children. Isn't that nice everyone?'

'Very nice' the visitors all shouted as they looked on expectantly, waiting for Olga to say a few words.

Olga took a deep breath and asked 'White wine or red please?'

The women and Othman opted for white while Nigel opted for red. After a few moments she brought in four bottles of white and two bottles of red. She placed the white wine in ice buckets situated at each corner of the table and placed the red in the middle of the table.

'Oh my God' exclaimed Nat looking at Jess. 'You don't expect us to get through this lot Jess, I mean, swan, do you?'

'Drink your fill
my little mouse
drink until you explode
But if you do please be warned
you'll end up in the road.'

Jess had obviously got this poetry thing down to a fine art while the others were struggling to keep up – the effects of alcohol were beginning to show.

'Fill your glasses everybody and let's have a toast.' They all stood up and raised their glasses.

'To old uni friends
and others from the past

Let's eat and drink and reveal ourselves
and enjoy this nightlong blast.'

Othman thought that Jess must've prepared and re-hearsed all these lines because no one, unless they were Lord Byron, could deliver such verse with such spontaneity. On reflection, he doubted whether even Byron could.

'Right my friends let's reveal ourselves. I'll go first. You'll never guess this but I'm'...Jess took off her mask and skull cap...'Jessica Garnett!'

'We would never have guessed' said Nigel.

'It's your turn Mrs cat' turning to Julia who took off her mask with a very realistic *meow*. Then the rest followed, unveiling themselves with sounds that ranged from a tiger's roar to a mouse's squeak. When it came to Othman's turn he pranced round the room like an ape, jumped on his chair and beat his chest before taking off his mask. He then screeched like a gorilla which made the ladies jump out of their skins – they were startled but, at the same time, impressed with what they saw after the unveiling. And so on until all the participants were unveiled.

'Right, welcome to you all. None of you have changed much – you all look so young and healthy. Okay, let me introduce my dear old uni mates – Natalie, Julia, Nigel and Othman.'

They each got up from their chair and took a bow, acknowledging each other at the same time.

'The other three gorgeous ladies did go to uni but I met them here in Wimbledon. We're known locally as the coffee set. How cool is that?'

'Very cool Jess' said Nat. 'But tell us about yourself - what did you do after uni?'

'I'll tell you after another toast my dear – it's a long story. Olga, I need you' she shouted, ringing the bell at the same time.

Meanwhile the members of the coffee set stood up and introduced themselves. They did this with varying degrees of confidence. June did her best but just wanted to get her introduction over and done with. Martha went on and on about her love for all things natural, and Joy monopolised the opportunity by spouting on about how many men and women she'd seduced in the last twelve months. Such an announcement caused a bit of a silence at first but this was soon followed by genuine laughter. Needless to say, they were all tipsy at this point having drunk three glasses of champagne and a glass of wine. And although June was quite reserved, Martha was less so, and Joy, who, having made her short speech, was beaming like a cheshire cat having assessed the quality of the opposite sex and, to a lesser degree, the young women from uni. At one stage, she wasn't far from bursting a blood vessel caused by her obvious excitement and over- zealous antics. These included a short strip tease routine which revealed her tanned six pack and a demonstration of back flips, hand-stands and squat bursts – the latter having Othman rolling on the floor in hysterics.

The party was going extraordinary well with people talking unreservedly and even cracking jokes about each other's mannerisms and demeanours. Olga kept them well oiled with wine and the first two courses went down very well. Time went by fast and people hadn't noticed that it was 11 pm.

Jess clicked her glass after the second course and announced that they must all participate in a party game. By this time everybody was getting quite rowdy so Jess rang her bell to get their attention. At the same time Olga rushed in and asked what was required.

'Nothing Olga, I'm just trying to keep this lot quiet. Listen everybody we're going to have a party game.'

Fortunately, the guests were so merry at this stage that none of them, not even June, objected. In fact June cried out: 'ooh, let's have a party game – I've got the pin, where's the donkey?' – she was beginning to lose her inhibitions!

'No June, not that kind of game – something a little more intellectual.'

'Trivial Pursuit' Othman shouted.

'No Othman, not Trivial Pursuit – something more personal.'

'Tell us more' said Joy.

'Right, what you've got to do is this: instead of each of us describing what we're like and what we've achieved over the last few years, I want the person opposite you, who should've got to know you by now in general terms, to guess what you're like and what you've achieved, and tell the rest of us.'

'Do we get a chance to interview each other first?' asked Martha.

'No Martha – just use your instincts.'

'What do you mean Jess – give us an example' said Nat.

'Okay, Okay. Suppose I'm describing you Nat.'

Jess stood up and motioned Natalie, who was at the other end of the table, to do the same.

'That should be easy because you know me from old.'

'Yes, I know that but it's just an example. Besides, it will be a bit of fun. I'll describe you and then you describe me.'

'Okay. Fire away.'

'Right. What I think I've found out about Nat is that she's got a good sense of humour and can put a poem together.'

Everybody laughed.

'I can tell by the way she dresses that she's got style and has probably done quite well for herself career wise.'

'So far so good Jess' said Nat.

'I know for a fact that she was great fun at uni even though she came from a poor background.'

Nat thought about this statement and said:

'Wait a minute Jess, what's a poor background got to do with having fun at uni. Are you saying that poor people can't have fun?'

'Of course not Nat, don't be so sensitive. You did really well considering.'

'Considering what?'

'That you were disadvantaged.'

'But I wasn't. I never complained about coming from a poor background.'

'I know you didn't dear, but I was lucky, my parents were well off so I could afford better clothes, better handbags and better shoes. You lot had to make do.'

'Us lot? What do you mean?'

'You know the poorer classes. Your parents and their parents had to work in factories and places like that. They had to work with their hands – blood sweat and tears – and all that hard graft. You probably had a loo in your back garden if, in fact, you had a back garden. Or was it called a yard? You suffered Nat, that's all I'm saying darling.'

'Yes we did, plus we had to put up with upper class twits like you' Nat said in a sharper tone.

'Now, now Nat' said Nigel 'keep it nice.'

'I'm only joking, of course, but it's true – you know you were a bit pompous Jess, especially when you had had a few.'

'May be so but at least I wasn't the village bicycle. You were at it most of the time Nat. I'm surprised the tops of your legs still meet.'

'I was enjoying myself, so what?'

'The word slag comes to mind.' Jess had gone too far...

Nat's body language and tone of voice changed. She became red in the face and her eyes took on a scary stare. She grabbed the table with both hands and pushed her chair back so it fell on the floor with a clutter.

'You arrogant rude bitch Jess, I'm going to slap you.'

'Oh no – handbags at dawn' Joy said trying to calm the situation down.

'It's my party Nat and I can say what I like. This is just like the old days. One minute we'd be fighting, the next we'd be partying.'

Nat was about to explode but then hesitated. What would losing her temper prove? After all, it was Jess's party and the food and drink had been good. Jess hadn't changed. She was still the pompous bitch and nothing was going to change that. She collected her thoughts and said:

'I know. Don't worry everybody. Jess and I have always been like this. We're a great double act. We rehearsed our banter for tonight so that we could liven up the party. Not that it needs livening up. Olga, can I have another wine?'

'Yeah. Drinks all round' said Jess. 'Now that everybody can see what this game is all about, let's start playing. Right, I'm first... Martha?'

'Yes?'

'I'll start with you. You are witty, self effacing, spoilt and generally, up in the clouds.'

'What?'

'As I said you're funny, you put yourself down a lot, you're supported by your parents and you love trees. That's about it. Now what do you think of me.'

Martha looked at Jess with astonishment. At that point she knew exactly what she thought of her. However, thankfully she was inebriated and was able to take Jess's comments with a pinch of salt. She decided though, having seen her mate in this state, that she would probably not be going to the next coffee morning get together. On the other hand, Othman was not so impressed and could see things getting out of control. He said:

'To be honest Jess, I don't think this game is working out. Let's play another game...how about sardines?'

'What's that?' asked June.

'Well, basically we see how many people can squeeze into a cupboard.'

'What's the point of that?'

'There's no point - it would just be a bit of fun and a way of getting to know each other. It would certainly be better than slagging each other off.'

They all looked at each other and laughed. Jess did have a knack of insulting people and then getting away with it, although the atmosphere in the room had become more tense despite the fact that most, if not all the guests were well over the limit.

At that point Olga brought out the desserts. There was a choice between mixed fruit salad and crème fraiche or crème caramel or lemon cheesecake. She placed all the dishes in the centre of the table so they could help themselves. Most of them took the mixed fruit and crème fraiche although the two men took the lemon cheesecake.

'Before we start' Jess said 'Another toast. Olga get the sweet wine from the fridge and fill all their glasses.'

Olga did what she was instructed and retreated back into the kitchen.

'Now fellow reprobates, I admit I'm pissed so if I insult you, which I probably will, don't take it seriously or personally. First to my husband – he supports me through thick and thin and obeys my every command. He's a wimp, but he's a rich wimp.'

'I hope he can't hear this Jess' said Julia.

'Of course he can't. He's listening to Brahms in his stupid man cave. Now, who's next. Oh yes. To Nigel who I once fancied but when I discovered he was also a wimp I decided to dump him.'

'That's not strictly true Jess. No one dumped anybody. We just parted company as we had nothing in common.'

'As I said I dumped Nigel cos he wouldn't fight like a man.'

'If you say so Jess' Nigel said realising that she was out of control.

Thirdly, Julia... I love Julia and there's nothing more to say. To Natalie, she was my rival in love and a 'good auld cockney sparrer.' To Othman, that devilishly handsome man from Africa or Egypt or from somewhere round there. To Joy, the over sexed bi and seducer of anything that moves. To Martha... well, you already know about her, and to June. What is there to say about quiet, timid June? I don't know so let's move on. Is anyone going to propose a toast to me, the housewife extraordinaire and beautiful hostess of this party?'

There was a pause.

'Yes I will' came a voice from outside the door leading to the hallway. Everybody went quiet.

They turned to look as Andrew made himself known to the party guests.

'Good evening everybody. I'm Jess's wimpish, rich husband and, although I'm not invited, I would like to make a toast to my beautiful wife.'

'Andrew' Jess snapped 'get back to your study – you're not part of this. You agreed.'

'Yes my darling, but I've changed my mind. I want to join in the fun. Here, let me have a sip of that sweet wine before I begin my speech.'

'Bravo Andrew' Nigel shouted. Let's give the man a chance.'

'Yeah' all the others (apart from Jess) cried.

'Good. But first let's start our desserts and while we're eating I will describe to you what an incredible woman my wife really is.'

Jess smelt a rat. Andrew wasn't normally like this. He'd obviously been drinking. She wanted to order him out but he had the majority vote. Andrew picked up a bowl containing the lemon cheesecake and pretended to eat it. The others dipped their spoons into the various dishes and began gorging themselves. After only seconds there was an outburst...

'What's this ?' cried Joy 'It tastes salty.'

'So does mine' said Othman.

'I'm going to be sick' shouted Martha.

'I've got to get to the bathroom' cried Julia as she fell off her chair and staggered towards the hallway. Andrew took one foot back to let her pass.

'I'm sorry Jess but this is revolting' said the normally timid June.

'Bit of a cock up on the home front Jess?' asked Natalie after she had spat the contents of her mouth into her bowl. 'Is this some kind of weird joke?'

'Shut up the lot of you' cried Jess who was now in a state of hysteria. 'These dishes were perfectly alright when I checked them this morning.' She turned to Andrew 'did you have anything to do with this ?'

'Perish the thought my little flower but while I've got your attention, let me just say this:

' I'm fed up being bossed around by you
– you treat me like a slave
Do the dishes clean the car
thank God I've got a cave.'

He paused. 'Did you like my little poem Jess? I composed it especially for you, my faithful wife.'

'What are you talking about Andrew. Be careful what you say.'

'Be careful what I say? That's rich coming from you my dear. I'd say you need to be careful what you *do*.'

The guests were now stunned into silence. Julia had returned from the bathroom and Olga had quickly removed all the desserts. The rest were gulping down the wine in an attempt to get rid of the awful tastes in their mouths. Andrew's little poem had caught their attention and now they were waiting for his next move – They all realised that the party was over but were curious to see how things would pan out. They were all drunk at this stage so the adrenaline was running wild and things were definitely hotting up.

'What do you mean, you foolish little man. I've done nothing wrong.'

'So you think that being unfaithful to your husband is Okay?'

'What are you talking about?'

'You don't know? Well I know all about your little affair.'

'Affair, what affair?'

'You know your affair with...' and before he could say another word, June let out a terrible scream.

They all turned to her. She had her mobile in her hand and stood there shaking from head to foot. She couldn't control her tears and wailed like a banshee. She was inconsolable. Joy put her arm round her and asked what was wrong.

'Luke is dead' she sobbed.

That night around 10 pm Luke had been making his way home after having a skinful with his mates. Among them was a girl called Lindsey who had recently joined the firm. Lindsey was young, attractive and the sort of girl Luke would go for. They'd both had a few too many and wandered out the pub around 9.15 pm.

'let's find a hotel Luke.'

'Haven't got time Linse, need to get home. How about down that alleyway?'

'You've got to be joking. I'm up for it but not down an alleyway. Who do you think I am, Nell Gwyn?'

'Who's she?'

'Doesn't matter. If that's the best you can do, I'm going home.'

'Okay, I'll walk you to the Bank.'

They parted company at Bank Station, Luke deciding that he would have a couple more pints before heading for Waterloo. He eventually caught the 10.30 to Raynes Park and staggered out of the train at around 11.00. By 11.10 he was facing his front door. He couldn't find his keys and spent some time rifling through his pockets. He wasn't too worried as June would still be at her dinner party which meant he wouldn't have to explain his lateness. At last he found his keys and then dropped them on the floor.

'Shit.' He said as he bent down to collect them. At that point he felt a terrible pain in his back. He tried to turn but as he did so felt a massive blow to his head. Everything blacked out after that. There was no pain anymore. In fact, there was nothing.

CHAPTER TEN

June, accompanied by Joy, rushed home by taxi and found that her front garden had been cordoned off. There were police cars, ambulances and people in white suits milling about outside her front door.

'Let me through she screamed, where's my husband?'

A tall policewoman put her arm round June and walked with her to the corpse. She uncovered Luke's face (which hadn't been affected by the attack, apart from the fact that he looked dead).

'Is this your husband sweetheart?' the policewoman asked in the most sympathetic tone she could muster.

'Yes, yes it's him. He can't be dead. He can't be' she wailed, and there was a short silence as the horrible sound echoed around the streets.

'I'm sorry sweetheart but they think he died about half an hour ago. Let's go into the house.'

June sobbed uncontrollably.

'I can't believe this is happening.'

'Can I phone anybody – a relative or a neighbour?'

'No, no I can't think at the moment.'

'Shall I make a cup of tea?'

'No. What happened?'

'Well, we got a call at around 11.30 saying there'd been an incident at your home address.'

'Who called?'

'We don't know, they wouldn't give their name to the switchboard. We assumed at first that it was just another hoax and thought nothing of it, but the girl on the switchboard thought otherwise so we got a police car down here straightaway.'

'But didn't they give any details?'

'Nope, they just said there'd been an incident and we'd better get ourselves down here'.

June put her head in her hands and wished that this was all a dream. She pinched herself several times in the hope she would wake up. But she was awake and this was no dream. Joy sat with her and held her hand. June couldn't stop shaking – her hands were sweaty and her mouth was dry.

'I can't bear this Joy, this can't be happening.'

'I know my love. This is a terrible shock.'

'How did he die?' she asked through tears. Joy offered her a tissue.

'It looks like he was attacked from behind with a knife and then hit on the head with a blunt but heavy instrument. Do you want to talk now? It would be great if you could because the faster we collect the facts, the faster we'll catch the murderer.'

Murder? June couldn't rationalise the situation. My husband's been murdered? she thought to herself - why? And who would want to kill him? After a couple of minutes she replied to the officer:

'Yes, yes of course. I'll tell you what I know. I'll try to anyway.'

'Where were you tonight Mrs ...'

'Masterson, my name is June Masterson. I was at a dinner party. Joy was there as well.'

'When did it start?'

'Oh... about 8 pm.'

'And when did you leave?'

'As soon as I got a phone call. This must've been around 11 to 11.30 pm I suppose. I was with seven other people including Joy. We were all a bit tipsy so I can't be sure.'

'Who phoned you.?'

'You guys?'

'Are you sure about that?'

'Yes, I think so. He said he was from the police. He had a slight Irish accent I think.'

'That's funny, we've no record of anyone from our lot making such a call. We didn't hear about this until after 11.30 pm. Everything's logged of course so we'll check the timings as soon as we can. You say he had an Irish accent?'

'Yes, I think so.'

'We don't have any Irishman at the station – not that I know of any anyway. How strange. Anyway how long have you been married?'

'About three years?'

'And what do you do?'

'I'm a biology lecturer – look what's this all got to do with my husband's death?'

'Just trying to complete the picture sweetheart. What did Luke do?'

'He was a trader at the Stock Exchange in the city.'

'Did he have any enemies?'

'No, at least not as far as I was aware. We were just a normal couple. Both had jobs. He sometimes worked late. He earned good money so we lived quite a luxurious life – no kids to worry about. No mortgage. We were perfect together – I can't believe this has happened.'

June started sobbing again and Joy put her arm round her. It was amazing how both of them had sobered up within the last forty minutes or so.

'So you have no idea why he was attacked?'

'None whatsoever.'

'You say your marriage was good?'

'Of course, why do you ask?'

'We have to cover every eventuality.'

'Was he ever on drugs?'

'No, he never went near the stuff. He liked a drink but so do all the city boys.'

'Of course. Well that's all I want to ask at this stage. No doubt a police inspector will be assigned to this case, so you can expect to be contacted again.'

'What happens now?'

'Well, the body will have to be taken to the mortuary. There will have to be a formal identification.'

'I've already identified him?'

'I know but that was in my presence. You will have to do it again down at the mortuary. The forensic boys will be analysing the wounds so that they can determine exactly how and when your husband died. Are you sure I can't contact someone for you – your mother, father...anybody?'

'No, both my parents are dead. If you could stay with me Joy, I'd appreciate it.'

'Of course I will my darling.'

'Right, I'll be off then. Are you sure there's nothing else you can tell me June...anything?'

'I can't think straight right now. I can't believe this has happened. Maybe tomorrow I'll think of something.'

'Okay, doubtless we'll be in touch tomorrow. See you later.'

As the officer approached the front door she stopped and turned around:

'Look, I'm terribly sorry about your husband - you have my deepest condolences. But whoever did this, whether it was a random attack or whether it was premeditated, the killer or killers won't get far because we have a witness.'

'A witness?' asked Joy.

'Yes, evidently one of the neighbours was woken up and saw two figures in June's front garden. He didn't actually see the full attack, or so I understand, but saw the two of them leave the premises and jump into a Ford Transit. He got the number plate.'

'Yes but they may have abandoned that van by now' said Joy.

'Yes, I know, but at least it's a lead. Goodnight ladies.'

June rushed to the front window and noticed that her husband's body was being taken away. She watched in silence. She was stunned and in total shock. Her front garden had been lit up by flashing blue headlights and she could see the lights from the house opposite. Obviously her neighbours were curious even though, apart from one, none of them had ventured forth to see what was going on.

June noticed that some curtains were closed while others were half open allowing the occupants to observe without being identified themselves. It would be different tomorrow – there would be police officers banging on every door asking questions about Luke's murder. 'Yes' June thought to her self – 'my husband has been murdered.' The realisation suddenly swamped her and she collapsed on the floor crying hysterically.

'Luke's dead, Luke's dead' she cried ' and he didn't even know I was pregnant.'

CHAPTER ELEVEN

Othman was summoned to the Assistant Chief's office. 'Sit down Oth got a job for you.'

'At last, what's that sir?'

'Well last night a Mr Luke Masterson was killed.'

'I know that.'

'You do. How ?'

'I was at a dinner party with his wife and six others. Nigel was there as well.'

'Tell me all.'

'All very innocent sir. It was a uni reunion. The hostess, Jess, shared a flat with Nige and I in our uni days. She invited us and another couple from uni. I'd never met June before, nor had Nige. She was just one of Jess's local friends.'

'Go on.'

'Well, not much else to say; round about 11.30 she gets a call. Next minute she's screaming her head off telling us that Luke's dead. She and her friend Joy took a taxi down to her house and the rest is history.'

'Didn't think of going yourself Oth?'

'Off duty sir. Besides we were pissed. June told us the message was from the police so we assumed the local bobbies were on the scene. Must admit, didn't think of checking the validity of the call at the time. It was all a bit of a shock and, as I've said, Nige and I were out of it. On reflection, perhaps we should have gone down there with her.'

'Perhaps you should've done but it wouldn't have made any difference. The time June got the call, whether it was the police or someone else, our victim had been dead for at least ten minutes.'

'Was there any trace of the villains?'

'A neighbour reckons he saw them and took a note of the number plate.'

'And?'

'Dead end. The van was picked up this morning. Forensics are working on it as we speak but the history of the vehicle doesn't give us much. The last owner was a builder from Exeter who died from a heart attack two weeks ago. '

'So do I get this case or not?'

'You do. Talk to the wife, the witness and Luke's mates at work – the usual stuff. I'll get the Devon boys to check out our dead friend in Exeter. I'll also check the telephone log to see whether any coppers phoned the wife at around 11.00 last night. Oh, and another thing – stupid me – check her mobile to track down the caller. Should have thought of that last night. Idiot that I am.'

'I'll do that first sir.'

'You won't be in conflict on this one Oth will you? I mean how well do you know June Masterson?'

'Don't know her at all. She was at the party but she barely spoke. I'd not met her before and I don't think we said anything to each other during the course of the whole evening.'

'Well apart from all that, you're not shagging her are you?'

'Get a life sir. It's not all about shagging nowadays.'

'Well, you know what I mean – handsome brute like you.'

'No, I have not shagged her, I don't know her and there's no conflict of interest – you have my word.'

'Then, get on with it.'

'Yes sir.'

'Oh and another thing, I'm off on holiday for a few weeks, they think I need a rest. The case is being handed down to the Superintendent – she's a bit of a Rottweiler so be careful.'

'No problem sir.'

Othman walked out into the main office and saw Nigel nursing a hangover. He explained that he'd been given the case and Nigel made out he was surprised. The truth of it was that Nigel had recommended Othman to take the case because he had successfully made the transition and was more than ready to solve his first crime on behalf of the Met. They agreed they would meet up after work for a couple of shandies as Nigel had been tasked with keeping an eye on the progress of the case. Although Chief inspector Othman was part of the team, he was still on secondment from the Cairo police and was still being watched by certain government officials. Such scrutiny was dissipating as time went by but Othman was still on the watch list, at least until the Iraq War was over – whenever that would be.

Othman made his way to June's address and parked his Ford outside her house. He was lucky to get a space this time of day as most roads around the Raynes Park area were filled with parked cars on both sides. The house was quite a large detached affair with a forecourt accommodating three cars. He rang the door bell and, within thirty seconds, he was facing a rather grand hallway.

'It's you' said Joy 'what do you want?'

'I've been assigned this case Joy and need to speak to June.'

'That's a bit strange. Shouldn't someone else be investigating Luke's murder?'

'Well we don't know for definite that it is murder – the forensics are working on Luke's body as we speak. They will confirm the estimated time of death and how he died as soon as they can. Until I speak to them, I'm keeping an open mind.'

'Well, evidently he had been bashed over the head and had a knife wound in his back – I don't see how that could have been an accident. Someone must have done it – he couldn't have done it himself!'

'You're probably right, but we must keep our options open. Now, where's June? Is she in a fit state to talk?'

'Yes, but you still haven't answered my question – why you?'

'Why not? I don't know June and I'm a fully qualified police officer. Besides, there's no one else available at the moment, so you'll just have to put up with me.'

Joy asked Othman to follow her and led him to the lounge where June was sitting on a leather sofa nursing a cup of tea and looking decidedly ill.

'I am so sorry about Luke June,' said Othman as he drew up a chair so he could be close to where she was sitting. 'This must be a terrible shock for you. I can't imagine what you're going through.'

'Thanks Othman. I don't know what to say or do. I feel helpless.'

'Are you up to speaking to me because I've been given this case to solve.'

'This case? Is Luke just *a case*? He was a human being, not *a case* Inspector... if that's your title.'

'No I'm sorry. I've been assigned to find out who killed your husband, always assuming that this is a murder case.'

'What else can it be? What do you want to know?'

'I got the low down from the officer who looked after you last night. Basically you received a call sometime between 11 and 11.30 pm last night. I know that because I was there. Who was the call from?'

'He said he was from the police?'

'Did he give a name?'

'No.'

'What did he sound like?'

'He had a slight Irish accent, I think.'

'Can I have your mobile June.'

'What for? don't you believe me? You were there for God's sake.'

'Yes I know and I do believe you of course, but we may be able to trace the caller.'

'But I told you, he said he was a police officer.'

'I know, but we don't have any record of any of our officers making such a call at that time of night. We certainly don't have anybody with an Irish accent.'

'It may have been someone from another station, or another area.'

'Yes that's true. We need to track down exactly who made that call so that we can be sure that it was a policeman who phoned you. If it wasn't, then we have to determine exactly who it was.'

June without hesitation handed over the phone and put her head in her hands. After a few minutes she gathered herself and asked Othman if he wanted a cup of tea. He accepted the offer as he had a few more questions to ask. Joy went into the kitchen to make some tea and brought back a tray supporting a teapot, jug of milk, three mugs and a plateful of chocolate biscuits. While she was occupied in the kitchen, Othman looked round the lounge. The decor wasn't particularly homely. There were no family photos nor any pictures, plants or other homely items which could generate a warm cosy atmosphere. The leather furniture had a polished orangey-red finish and the vinyl flooring was a cheap imitation of yellowy pine wood. The coffee table was constructed of glass and hadn't been cleaned for some time. Othman got the impression that June and Luke used their accommodation as a house rather than a home and probably devoted most of their time to their careers, caring little about the finer details of domestic life. He wondered how close they really were. He then stopped himself because he was jumping to conclusions – they may have been blissfully happy – and the way June was conducting herself suggested that this was, in fact, the case.

'I'll put the tray down here. I'll leave you to pour your milk. I've assumed you don't take sugar?'

'Correct' Othman said and turned to June.

'How long did you know Luke June?'

'About six years. We met at a party. Well, it wasn't a party as such – it was in a pub near my university. I'd finished work and a few of my colleagues decided to go to the pub. Luke was there with his city mates. I didn't notice him at first but then this big guy came over and offered me a drink. The rest is history.'

'What did you know about what he did in the city?'

'Very little. I knew he was a trader and had been very successful, but I never got too involved. I wasn't interested in the money markets. We struck up a good relationship as I was hopeless with money while he was brilliant. We had a joint account which I rarely used. I let him deal with all the statements and when I needed money, he would let me have it. To be honest Othman, I was happy to let him provide for me while I concentrated on my career.'

'You're a biology lecturer?'

'That's correct. I've been promised promotion to head of department next term so I've tended to focus on my job rather than worry about domestic stuff. We usually eat take-aways if we're at home but mostly we eat out. Oh my God I'm talking as if he's still alive. He's gone and I can't believe it.'

June started crying again and Joy put her arm round her to comfort her.

'I'm sorry June. I know this is very raw. If you want me to stop, I will.'

'No, no. We might as well get this over with.'

'I know this might be a strange question, but did you get on with each other? Did you have a good relationship?'

'What sort of question is that? Of course we did. He was my world. I loved him very much. Sure there would be nights when he came home late from work, sometimes drunk, sometimes not, but we never had any serious rows. We were happy with the way we lived. He didn't interfere with my work and I didn't interfere with his. It worked.'

'When did you last see him alive?'

'Yesterday morning. He was in a hurry to get to work. I t was always busy on a Friday, or so he said, and he had plans to go out with his mates after work. He knew I was going to a dinner party so I guessed we'd meet up later in bed.'

'What did he say to you?'

'The usual stuff - have a good day, see you later. Love you – all that kind of thing. He then kissed me and left.'

'Nothing unusual?'

'Not at all.'

'Did he ever not come home at night?'

'No, never.'

'What do you know about his friends and work colleagues ?'

'Very little. He mostly devoted his life to me. He occasionally played golf with his old school mates and went for a drink after work, but, apart from that, he didn't socialise much – he had too much work to do as a trader. In any case, that's what he told me and I believed him.'

'Do you know the names of any of his mates outside or inside work?'

'There's only one guy he's ever mentioned.'

'And who's that?'

'A guy called Grant at work.'

'Do you now his surname?'

'No, but Luke often mentioned him. They were evidently good drinking buddies.'

'Okay, could you give me the name and address of your husband's company.'

June got up and went to a pinewood desk in the corner of the room. She took out a bunch of papers from one of the drawers and placed them on the coffee table. She then started sifting through them until she found a piece of headed paper with the name and address of Luke's employers - Albion PLC Threadneedle Street, London. She handed this over to Othman and continued sifting through the papers. She'd never opened this desk before as she knew it contained all Luke's work papers and accounts, and had no interest, inclination or, indeed, need to look through this documentation. Things had changed now and she prepared herself for what lay ahead. She therefore carried on looking. At the bottom of the pile she found a statement of their joint account. She studied it:

'Oh my God' she screamed, we're in debt.'

'Can I have a look ?' asked Othman.

June handed over the statement and Othman was startled to see that the Mastersons were in debt by over £6000.

'Did you know anything about this June?'

'Not a thing. Luke always paid me in cash.'

'Have you any savings or did you just have this one account?'

'We had separate accounts as well and I have been able to save up some money, although not much – my salary was automatically transferred into the joint account.'

'Thank God you've got some money' Joy said. 'You need to get hold of your solicitor straightaway.'

'Joy's right June' said Othman. 'You're going to need help to sort out your financial matters from now on. You'd better check every nook and cranny in this house for statements, letters and bills relating to Luke's affairs. It'll be a tough job, but you've got to do it. Let me know as a matter of urgency what you find – anything and everything relating to Luke will be of paramount importance in our investigations.'

Othman got up to go.

'Oh, and by the way, did Luke have an enemies or anybody he fell out with – either in or out of work?'

'I don't think so. He never mentioned anything like that. He was looking a bit stressed in recent months but I put that down to his job. As I said before, occasionally he would come home drunk, but he was a happy drunk. Not the sort of drunk who was aggressive. He never talked about arguments or fights or revenge. He was generally a happy soul – drunk or sober. I'm sure he had no enemies.'

'Were you ever suspicious that he might be having an affair?'

'Never in a million years. We were right for each other. It has never entered my head. He was the perfect husband as far as I was concerned. Everybody loved him. I'm surprised you're asking me these questions Inspector.'

'Have to June. Got to explore every avenue.'

'I know, but what I haven't told you is that I've just found out I'm pregnant with Luke's child. That shows that he loved me and no one else, doesn't it?'

'Of course' Joy said 'he only had eyes for you my dear.'

'One last question and I want you to answer this honestly – both of you. Was Luke a good looking man, you know the sort of man who was universally handsome and attractive to women?'

Without thinking both of them nodded their heads.

'He was one of the most attractive men I'd ever come across' said Joy. ' But of course, he was strictly out of bounds. Besides he was besotted with June – you could see that when they were together.'

'I see. Okay ladies thank you for your help and I will be in touch. Once again June I' m so sorry for your loss.'

CHAPTER TWELVE

Jessica sat on the end of her bed nursing a rather nasty hangover. After June and Joy had left the party the other guests quickly took their leave with solemn looks on their faces. The party had been a disaster! What a time for Luke to die – right in the middle of the entertainment. And Andrew – what was he trying to prove? He'd never shown an interest to verse before! As she was pondering on these rather bizarre thoughts, Andrew, who had spent the night, as he often did, in the spare bedroom, burst into the room:

'Well Jess. What have you got to say for yourself? I know you've been having an affair with Luke Masterson and now he's ended up dead. What an earth is going on?'

'I haven't had an affair with him and I don't know anything about his death.'

'Don't lie. I've suspected for some time you've been playing around so I hired a detective to follow you.'

'You what?'

'You heard. I've got photographs of you and Luke entering and leaving a hotel in Sutton. What were you doing there? Playing tiddly winks?'

'It's nothing like that, I promise you.'

'So there was something going on?'

'You're bluffing – there are no photographs.'

Andrew left the room and returned with a large brown envelope. He spread the photos across the bed. They showed ten scenes in which Jess and Luke were either entering different hotels or entering his car. One photograph showed them kissing on Wimbledon Common.

'Look Jess, if I'm not mistaken that's you and that's Luke. You'd better have some very good explanations otherwise you'd better prepare yourself for an ugly divorce.'

Jess changed her demeanour. She'd been found out. She saw her whole lifestyle being seriously threatened and decided to play the remorseful wife who'd lost her way:

'Oh darling please forgive me. The truth is I was getting bored at home. You were out at work all the time and we've had no time to talk things through. We rarely see each other and I just wanted an escape from my humdrum life. I'm so sorry, please understand. It was just sex – nothing else. There was no love or affection. In fact even before he died I'd called it off – I knew it was wrong and I realised how much you'd meant to me.'

'What utter bullshit. Don't you remember – I'm the rich wimp who's at your beck and call. Sure, you like my money because it provides you with a high standard of living, but that's about it – you show me no respect or affection. I might as well be your slave.'

'I'll change. This has made me realise how much I love you. There was no love between me and Luke. He was just a means to an end – someone to fill in the time while you were away.'

'This is getting worse. Look Jess you've been caught in the act and I'm still waiting on your explanations.'

'I've given them to you. I can't say anything else. I'm sorry and it won't happen again.'

'I don't care if it does. We're finished so you better pack your bags. You can stay with your mother.'

'Please let me stay a few days to sort myself out?'

'Of course. That will give us time to talk about Luke's death. Do you know anything about this? You'd better tell me all because if you don't I'm going to phone the police. They'll probably want to talk to you anyway but it might be a good idea if you tell me everything, and I mean everything, before they start their investigations.'

'Okay, give me a chance to get dressed and I'll tell you everything.'

'You'd better Jess. Right now I'm thinking we're all over but I'll give you a chance to explain yourself. And another thing, if I allow you to stay, there will be a few changes round here. From now you will do what I say and you can forget about your luxurious lifestyle.'

'Okay, I understand and I deserve everything you throw at me. But, for the sake of the kids, please let me stay?'

'I'll consider that later – not that you've been a caring mother. Up to now the kids haven't exactly been in the fore-front of your thoughts – you care more about your own particular lifestyle. No Jess, you better make this good because we are at the end of the line. I'm no longer the wimp – you'd better believe me.'

Andrew got up and made for the door.

'Wait a minute Andrew I might as well tell you now. Luke told me he was into drug dealing. He offered me some but I refused. He then told me that he owed one of his colleagues a lot of money and asked whether I would lend him 20K. I told him I couldn't and immediately ended the affair.'

'Do you remember the name of his colleague?'

'I think it was Grant Malley or was it O'Malley, I can't remember precisely. Any way that's it. I didn't see him again.'

'But you would have kept seeing him had he not mentioned anything about the drugs – wouldn't you?'

'No it would have ended any way.'

'I don't believe you Jess. Anyway it doesn't matter now. We're finished. I'm going to call the police.'

CHAPTER THIRTEEN

Othman and Lucy managed to get together that week and did something they had never done before – went to the opera. They met on the steps of the National Gallery and gazed across Trafalgar Square for a good ten minutes. There were several pavement artists performing a variety of acts which included a man and his dog on stilts playing a ukulele and a woman painted green on a unicycle playing the saxophone and occasionally singing verses from the National Anthem. On the other side of the square were buskers of various sorts including a multi-instrumental act involving an old man playing a guitar, mouth-organ and nose flute while, at the same time, beating time with symbols attached to his knees. It was an incredible sight and his partner, who looked about as old as he, mingled with the crowd asking for money using a bowler hat as a collection box. Nearer to where Othman and Lucy were standing were two girls performing mime in red outfits. They looked like they were depicting a scene from a Punch and Judy show as one was holding a truncheon while the other was holding a doll which was supposed to be a baby. It wasn't too clear as to what they were trying to convey, but their balletic moves and actions were sufficiently dramatic to attract a small, appreciative crowd which cheered every time the doll dodged the truncheon. Both Othman and Lucy felt the act was a bit bizarre and walked slowly away towards the Coliseum Theatre. Not discouraged by such exits the red duo continued their miming antics until the crowd completely dispersed, at which point they flung their props to the floor and took enjoyment from their previously prepared rolled-up cigarettes. Such were the eccentricities of a city which had grown over many centuries and produced street performers who, perhaps, at one time, yearned for the stage but found themselves instead expressing their natural talent on the pavement. Whether on the stage or on the pavement, these people were skilful and desirous of entertaining the public in a city which loved to be entertained.

Othman had upper circle tickets for the evening performance of Puccini's Tosca. He had heard this man's music before and, unlike other operas, had been impressed by the romantic melodies and colourful orchestral compositions which provided a light entertainment rather than a heavy hard to follow depressing one. The theatre was very impressive with elaborate carvings, chandeliers, balconies and an overall decor which gave a victorian feel. Othman and Lucy were high up and had an excellent view of the stage and could just make out some of the members of the orchestra. Neither of them had been to the opera before and didn't know what to expect. However, they quickly became absorbed in the atmosphere and waited patiently for the first singer to burst into song. They were not disappointed. Every performer had an incredible voice and the two of them were able to follow the story line by reading the translation displayed on a screen above the stage. Othman followed the gist of the plot which involved a painter giving refuge to an escaped political prisoner; his jealous and suspicious wife, Tosca; her killing of a rather nasty and lecherous persecutor; and their final demise involving the painter's execution and her falling off the back of the stage! The tragic story unfolded with wonderful vocal performances supported by dramatic acting gestures which, Othman assumed, were all part of the total operatic experience. The two of them were impressed with the quality of the production and, after the third and final act, decided to celebrate with a drink in a nearby pub.

'Poor Tosca. She was so suspicious but had nothing to worry about. He truly loved her. What was the painter's name?' Lucy asked Othman.

'His name was Mario Cavaradossi.'

'And what about that horrible man?'

'The chief of police was called Scarpia and reminded me of some of the chiefs I've worked for!'

'Well, he ended up dead at the hands of a woman.'

'Yes, *hell hath no fury*, and all that good women's liberation stuff.'

'Absolutely right. He had it coming, the bastard.'

'Now, now Lucy, not all women would stab a guy in the stomach just because he made a move on them.'

'Some move – he was trying to rape her!'

'True but he had agreed to let her lover go if she allowed him to have his way with her.'

'But it was the way he handled the situation. I don't blame her for killing him.'

'Well, I suppose, it was the right thing to do in the end as he double crossed her. No way was he going to let Mario get away with hiding a political figure, so he was prepared to lie in order to get his way with her. He got his just desserts.'

'Any parallels Oth?'

'All the time – as you know. Got a case at the moment where a murder has been committed in Raynes Park. I was at a dinner party with the wife whose husband got killed. You can bet your life there's some serious lying going on.'

'Tell me more.'

'Nothing more to tell. I didn't know the woman and it was pure coincidence that I was at the party when her husband died. She reckoned she got a call from a copper but we can't trace such a call. As far as she's concerned, he had no enemies and is at a loss as to why it happened.' There was a pause. 'Another strange thing though is that they shared a joint account. She thought they had plenty of money but was horrified when she found out they were, in fact, heavily in debt.'

'But he must have had some enemies. Either that or it was a pure random killing dished out by some psycho.'

'Not psycho Luce – someone with mental disabilities or, better still, someone with learning difficulties. They're the great definitions nowadays, I believe? Either way, the poor man is dead and I've got to find the murderer.'

'You? Why you? You were at the party. Couldn't someone else be given the task?'

'I wasn't the only copper. Nigel Francis was also there so, in theory, he could've been given the case. But, you see, we assumed when she got the call, it was someone from the Met. We assumed it was being handled by another copper. Turns out that may not be the case and my chief is anxious to give me a task so that I can get my teeth into something. Nigel will be behind the scenes making sure I don't cock up. You know the background don't you?'

'Yeah, you told me you were on secondment from the Cairo police and that you'd been involved in some political scam involving MI5. You didn't give me the details.'

'Nor shall I Luce – it's all too fraught and better you stay out of it. Anyway, I was given the case so I could prove myself. There's no conflict of interest as I had and have no connections with the mourning wife.'

'Poor lady.'

Just as Othman had finished his second pint his mobile rang. It was Andrew Garnett.

'Is that Mr Othman?'

'Just Othman or Inspector Othman.'

'Well, hello. I'm Andrew Garnett, Jessica's husband.'

'Yes, I remember you. You were making an interesting speech when June got the phone call.'

'That's right. If that phone call hadn't happened, I'm sure the party would've come to an abrupt end in any case.'

'Maybe you're right. It was definitely heading that way.'

'Any way, Jess and I may have some information which may be relevant. Can we see you?'

'Of course. How about tomorrow afternoon at 2 pm? I'm interviewing a witness in the morning but could make the afternoon.'

'That would be fine. See you then.'

Othman switched off his phone and put his arm round Lucy. They gave each other a quick kiss and made their way towards the exit. It had been raining for the last hour or so but as they walked towards Trafalgar Square, the rain eased off. London at night after a bout of heavy rain looked beautiful. The lights from the cars and neon signs made the pavements glisten. The streets were full of different colours which seemed to intensify after the rain had washed the grime away. As usual, the area was packed with people, mostly young, who were on their way to a pub or, better still, a 'rave' where they would get high on either alcohol or drugs, it didn't matter which, and then stagger off home, without a care in the world, in the early hours of the morning. Later they would be nursing a hangover but, as they were young, this would soon pass and they would prepare themselves for another night of 'devil-may care' en-joyment. Not all youngsters were like this of course, but as a copper Othman was already becoming cynical and tending to look on the pessimistic side when it came to pondering on the future of Britain's youth - and its desire for instant self –gratification. It seemed to Othman that youngsters no longer had the patience to wait for a good time to happen. They had to have the good times now and, with the availability of limitless credit, they could fulfil these needs thinking there would be no end to being able to finance their various enterprises. The thought of actually saving up enough money to finance a 'good time', and waiting until such sufficient funds had accumulated, was a thought that never entered the minds of many young people. Othman thought that one day the bubble would burst and the cash machines would be out of money. The 'live now pay later' philosophy would then become a reality – but not in a good way. With this in mind he and Lucy decided to walk to Vauxhall rather than catch a cab!

CHAPTER FOURTEEN

The next day Othman made his way to Raynes Park to speak to the main witness. According to the duty officer, Mr Martin Parks was a big man in his sixties. A successful builder by trade, he'd paid off his mortgage and lived in a detached house opposite June Masterson. Othman noticed that the house had been extended quite considerably. It looked like Parks had converted the loft and had turned the garage into a dining room, extending upwards to create, perhaps, a fifth bedroom. On the other side of the house he'd built a car port which accommodated his van. In the forecourt, which had recently been paved, he had erected a fountain which was not in operation at the time Othman pressed the buzzer located on the front gate. As he waited he surveyed the west side of the forecourt which accommodated two cars – a BMW and a Nissan Micra.

A voice came through the speaker:

'Who is it?'

'Inspector Othman. I've come about the incident which occurred the other night.'

'Oh, you'd better come in then.'

Parks released the gate and Othman went up to the front door. By the time he'd climbed the final step the door was opened by a young attractive girl in her thirties dressed only in her dressing gown. She was heavily made up, especially around her eyes - as if she were trying to hide something, and her blonde hair had been sternly combed back revealing a shiny forehead with remnants of face cream showing on her temples. The dressing gown hung loose exposing a little too much bosom, part of which had been tattooed with what looked like a snake curled round a cross. She held a little hairy miniature thing which looked more like a rat than a dog

'Come in Inspector. Do you want tea or coffee?'

'No thanks. Just had some.'

'Would you mind taking your shoes off. I don't know why we bought a cream carpet but Martin was insistent. He thinks it adds class to the hallway or something like that. Anyway come through and sit down.'

Othman quickly tried to determine whether this girl was Park's wife or daughter. He looked round for photographs but could see none. As he was trying to figure out the relationship, Parks came in:

'You've met my partner. I'm Martin Parks, pleased to meet you.'

'Hi, I'm Chief Inspector Othman.'

'How can I help ?'

Othman got his notebook out and searched for his pen. He couldn't find it and Parks offered him a cheap biro.

'Right. Thanks. What did you see the other night? Tell me everything you know.'

'Okay, it was around 11.15 pm when I heard a noise. Me and the missus were having our last glass of wine and were just about to go to bed.'

'What sort of noise?'

'It was a van or lorry. I thought, strange at this time of night so I went up to the bedroom and moved the curtains so I could get a better look. The van stopped. I then noticed a figure walking down the road. It was Luke. I knew it was him. Luke's a big fella – you can't miss him. Besides, the street lights were on so I saw his face. He went up to his front door. He must've dropped something cos he went on his knees looking around on the floor. Within a split second these two blokes – well I assume they were blokes - jumped out of the van. They had their backs to me so I didn't see their faces. They were dressed in black. Big guys. You know what I mean. Next minute I hear a scream and there's a struggle going on. I see one of them hit Luke on the head with what looked like an iron bar. I thought to myself – Oh my God. In a split second they left leaving Luke lying on the floor and got into their van and drove away. I managed to get the number and gave it to you lot.'

'Couldn't you do anything to stop it?'

'Not in a million years – it happened so quick. It was over within seconds.'

'What did you do next?'

'I phoned you lot of course.'

'Did you go down to see what'd happened?'

'No.'

'Why not?'

'Didn't want to disturb anything. Besides, I knew the police would be down in a minute.'

'That's strange behaviour Mr Parks?'

'Look Inspector, we all mind our own business round here. I didn't want to get involved. I'd done nothing wrong. There's no law that says you've got to attend to a body. Besides Liz my partner phoned for an ambulance so there was nothing else we could do.'

'You might've saved his life?'

'I don't know any first aid. I wouldn't have known what to do. I may have even made it worse. Look

Inspector it's not me that's the villain. It's those two that did it. You'd be better spending your time looking for them rather than coming round here accusing me of things.'

'I'm not accusing you of anything. It just seems a bit sad that you didn't do anything.'

'As I said, I didn't want to get involved.'

'How long have you known the Mastersons?'

'Not very long. They've only been in that house a couple of years. People don't talk to each other much round here. We say hello. I've chatted to Luke before. He was a nice bloke.'

'What was he like?'

'As I said, he was a nice bloke. Worked in the city. Wasn't posh or anything. Good looking bloke. I think my missus fancied him but she knows she's on to a good thing with me and wouldn't step out of line – if you know what I mean Inspector.'

'Where was your wife when all this happened?'

'She was getting ready for bed. She didn't hear anything.'

'Can I speak to her?'

'Sure, Liz, can you come here darling.'

Liz had got dressed and was wearing ultra tight jeans with a yellow tee shirt. She knew how to move her body and wiggled into the lounge holding her little dog in her arms. Othman noticed further tattoos on her hands and wrists. Parks noticed Othman looking and said:

'Don't be fooled Inspector. My Liz likes her tattoos but she's no ignorant slag if that's what you're thinking.'

'I'm not thinking that at all Mr Parks. I was just trying to figure out what the tattoos show.'

'This one's a dying swan and this one's a gargoyle' she said.

'Oh yes. I can see that now. Very nice.'

'Do you want to see the one I've got on my arse Inspector?'

'Not really Mrs Parks.'

'I'm not Mrs Parks Inspector. Just call me Liz.'

'Fine. Did you call for an ambulance the other night?'

Liz looked furtively at Parks who lowered his eyes.

'Yes, yes I did' she said hesitantly.

'What time was this?'

'About 11.15, 11.30, not sure.'

'Okay Liz. Do you know June from across the road?'

'Not really. We speak in the street sometimes when I'm going to yoga but apart from that we don't meet.'

'Have you detected any problems over there?'

'What do you mean?'

'Well, did they appear happy together? Were there any fights or arguments?'

'None that I saw Inspector. They were a normal couple as far as I know.'

'Did you know the husband Luke Masterson?'

'Yes, I knew him and I've spoken to him before. Again, in the street as we passed each other by.'

'Have you ever been into their house – you know for coffee or tea.'

'Never' said Liz.

'Did he ever come on to you Liz?'

'Now wait a minute Inspector' interjected Parks 'what are you saying?'

'Let Liz answer Mr Parks.'

There was a long pause as Liz tried to think.

'No, I would say no'. She paused again and was about to say something but then hesitated...

'You were going to say Liz?'

'Well, he would smile at me if he saw me and I would smile back. Just being polite to each other – nothing more.'

'Are you sure?'

'Of course I'm sure. If you're suggesting I'd had an affair with him you're wrong and bang out of order.'

'I've never suggested that. I'm just trying to gauge how well you knew the Mastersons and especially Luke.'

'Well I've told you. We were neighbours and nothing more.'

'Is there anything else either of you can tell me?'

'There's nothing to tell' said Parks.

'Very well. If you think of anything, then let me know. Here's my card.'

'Is that it? asked Parks. Will you want to speak to us again?'

'Why do you ask Mr Parks. Do you think I'll need to?'

'No, of course not. Just saying.'

'Fine. If I need to speak to you again, I will. Meanwhile, please don't leave the country.'

'But we're going to Lanzarote next week.'

'Fine, give me the details and there'll be no problem. Phone this number today and they'll make a note of the dates of travel and the hotel you're staying in. Oh and I better take both your mobile numbers just in case we need to discuss the situation again. I'll see my own way out.'

'Wait a minute Inspector. Can I have my pen back?'

'Sure. Here it is. Goodbye.'

'You lied Liz, you did have a fling with him didn't you?'

'I know but we agreed I'd keep quiet. I kept quiet about everything. Please don't hit me again. I've said I'm sorry. It won't ever happen again I promise you.'

Parks became angry as the Inspector's visit had reminded him of his partner's infidelities. He rose from the armchair and grabbed Liz's arm. His face reddened and he looked as though he would burst. He stared at her with a manic look in his eyes – he looked like Robert Newton, the actor, who starred in the fifties as *Long John Silver*. He said in a stern, threatening and yet controlled way:

'Well, it won't happen again with Luke will it you filthy whore. If I find out you're carrying on with anyone else, I'll give you another black eye and you'll be out on your nice little arse. Meanwhile, do what I say and don't tell the police anything. Do you understand my pretty little Lizzy?'

Parks grabbed her by the throat and squeezed.

'Of course I understand' she croaked 'please let me go.'

He let her go and she went running to her room.

CHAPTER FIFTEEN

Othman drove round to Jess's house and parked his car in a side turning. He was parked on a double yellow so placed his identification card on the dashboard. He had about an hour to waste so decided to have a coffee in the *Dog and Fox*. This pub was popular with the Met and Othman was bound to bump into someone he knew. He took his cup of coffee over to a quiet corner and phoned Nigel on the off chance he might be in the neighbourhood. He was and the two of them agreed to meet in the pub.

After about 10 minutes Nigel turned up and Othman explained that he had visited the prime witness – Martin Parks, and had taken down statements for both Parks and his partner, Liz. He told

Nigel that he didn't believe a word Liz had said and suspected that she was under pressure to lie from Parks. He suspected that she'd had a fling with Luke Masterson, Parks found out and gave her a hard time - maybe even assaulting her. This being the case Parks had a motive to kill Luke and must therefore be regarded as a suspect. Nigel followed the reasoning but pointed out the existence of the van – why would Parks give evidence relating to this vehicle and, indeed, why would he provide details of the assault, when he in fact was the murderer or had something to do with the murder? Why would he incriminate himself? Othman thought for a moment and suggested that he did this to distract the police away from himself. Either that or he hired two contractors to do his dirty work for him. Whatever the circumstances, if Parks were a suspect, he was playing a risky game because by identifying the van used by his contractors as a distraction strategy, such a disclosure could result in serious reprisals. They both agreed that a lot of this analysis was conjecture and that further investigations would have to be undertaken before any arrests were made. Nigel also questioned whether a man like Parks – a successful builder, nice home, nice set up etc. would really want to kill his partner's lover. It seemed like a step too far – given all the circumstances. Othman agreed. Nevertheless, they left it that Parks could be a suspect and, there-fore, another visit was probably necessary. Othman phoned up the station to check whether Parks had handed in his holiday details. He was relieved to find that he had.

They decided that they would visit Jess and her husband, Andrew, together. Othman would take the lead and Nigel would take notes. There may have been a conflict of interest if Nigel got too involved bearing in mind his relationship with Jess in their uni days. However, the relationship didn't exactly take off and the risk of there being a conflict several years later was small, to say the least. To be on the safe side, just in case Jess decided to use that card, it was agreed that Nigel would keep out of it. Having said this, there was good reason why he should be present as he had been tasked with supporting Othman and there was no reason why they couldn't work together in this way. What Othman didn't know was that he was still being watched by the pow-ers that be and his mate Nigel had been assigned to undertake such a brief, reporting back if, for any reason, Othman veered off from his investigations or got himself entangled in any political row. This, of course, was unlikely because this particular case looked straight forward enough – it certainly didn't involve governmental politics or MI5 intervention – at least that's what Nigel believed.

They parked their cars in the forecourt and the sound of rubber on gravel must have been heard by Andrew who opened the front door as they exited their respective cars.

'Good afternoon gentlemen. I thought there would be just one of you but we are honoured to have two of you at our doorstep. Do come in.'

'Thanks' said Othman. 'Nigel's here to take notes – nothing else. I will be asking all the questions if, in fact, there are any questions to be asked.'

'I'm sure there will be, but do come into the lounge. Jess is waiting for us there. Tea or coffee gentlemen?'

'Coffee white with no sugar' they both said.

'Fine. Look who's arrived Jess – your old uni friends. How nice for everyone.'

Jess sat on the sofa looking decidedly haggard. She hadn't put any make up on and her hair was in a mess. She looked as though she'd lost weight and there were dark circles under her eyes. She appeared to have re-signed herself to her fate – whatever that might be – and hadn't the energy to resurrect her bubbly, slightly annoying, some would say disturbing, personality. She held a mug of tea in both hands and studied the contents rather than engage in greeting formalities.

'Now come on Jess, these kind policemen friends of yours want to talk to you. You can at least give them a smile.'

'There's nothing to smile about'

Othman sat down opposite her and Nigel took up position in an armchair, note pad and pen at the ready.

'Now what do you want to tell us Jess?' Othman asked.

'Go on Jess. Tell him everything otherwise I will' Andrew said as he made his way towards the kitchen.

'I was having an affair with Luke. He told me he was part of a drug dealing ring and owed his mate a lot of money. He asked me whether I could bail him out and I said no. I then ended the affair and never saw him again. That's the long and short of it Inspector Othman.'

'Do you know the name of his mate?'

'It was Grant someone or other.'

'Grant O'Malley?'

'That's right Grant O'Malley. They were supposed to be great friends at work.'

'Do you know anything about Luke's murder Jess?'

'Not a thing, I promise you. I knew he was in trouble and told him to sort himself out. I didn't know he was going to end up dead.'

'What do you know about this Grant O'Malley?'

'Only what Luke told me. I've never met him and don't particularly want to.'

'Why's that?'

'Because he sounds like a complete thug. He was providing drugs to Luke who was supposed to sell the stuff on. Trouble is, Luke told me, he'd become addicted and consumed a lot of the product. That's why he came to me. He wanted to sell the stuff to me so that he could make some money. When I said no, he told me everything.'

'How much did he ask you for?'

'20K.'

'Do you know whether he had been threatened by Grant in any way?'

'I don't know for sure but I expect he was. Funny though, well, it's not funny; the last thing he said to me was that he'd probably end up dead in the gutters.'

'What did you say to that?'

'I told him not to be so melodramatic and to sort himself out. I never believed for one minute that it would end up like this. I thought he was just playing the poor victim in the hope of getting my sympathy. I certainly didn't give him any – perhaps I should have done, I don't know.'

Andrew returned with the coffees and handed them out. He sat down in an armchair opposite Nigel.

'Well dear. Have you told them everything?'

'As much as I know.'

'Do you think that Grant O'Malley killed Luke?' asked Othman.

'He may have done. He had a motive. He wanted his money back. If it wasn't him it may have been someone he knew. Even though he was a drugs dealer, according to Luke, he held down a good job at the Exchange. I can't imagine someone like that wanting to risk it all by killing a colleague. As I said maybe he got one of his shady mates to do it. I don't know. I wasn't involved, thank God.'

'Thanks Jess. Unless you can tell us anything more, we'll make a visit to our friend at the Exchange or wherever he works. I've got the address.'

'How did you get that?' asked Andrew.

'June found some papers in a drawer. She also found out for the first time that they were heavily in debt.'

'Poor June. Does she know that her husband was having an affair with me?'

'No. The only thing she knows is that her husband is dead.'

'Can we keep it like that?'

'I see no reason why we can't. We're only concerned with Luke's murder, always assuming it was murder.'

'What else could it be?'asked Andrew.

'It could have been an accident. It may even have been suicide. We're keeping our options open. But you're right – all things point to murder.'

'For the last time Jess – do you know anything more about Luke's murder?'

'No Othman, I've told you everything I know.'

'Well, if you think of anything else, no matter how small, please contact me. Here's my card. Right Nige, lets pay our old friend O'Malley a little visit.'

'Right boss. You lead the way' said Nigel.

The two of them took their leave and sped towards the city. They wanted to catch O'Malley before he left work. They activated their sirens to show the world they meant business!

'I'm glad that's over Andrew' said Jess.

'Yes my dear. Now we have to discuss that little matter of our marriage.'

CHAPTER SIXTEEN

It was about 4.30 in the afternoon and Threadneedle Street was beginning to buzz with the first signs of the daily rush-hour. Bankers, traders, executives and all the other city slickers were making their way to either an underground station or to a local pub. From 5 to 7 the 'happy hour' reigned in most pubs during which many young executives got slaughtered before making their way home. Their jobs were highly stressful (or so we're told) and some kind of relief had to be found, and this usually took place in a pub or a wine bar.

Othman and Nigel parked illegally in one of the side turnings and ran towards the office in which, it was hoped, Grant worked. Othman asked a security guard the whereabouts of O'Malley and was directed towards the fourth floor. Nigel pressed the buzzer and the receptionist released the door.

'Is Grant O'Malley around?' Othman asked a surprisingly old receptionist.

'Who shall I say is here?'

'Othman, Inspector Othman from the Metropolitan Police.'

'Oh I see. I'll give him a call. Could you sign the book please gentlemen.'

The receptionist made the call and turned round to Othman:

'Mr O'Malley said he cannot speak to you today as he has to finish work early.'

Nigel politely took the phone from the receptionist's hand and whispered:

'Get your arse down here O'Malley, there's a good chap. We don't want to cause any fuss now do we?'

'Who's that?' came the reply.

'Inspector Francis – you remember me don't you Grant?'

'How can I forget. Alright, be down in a mo.'

'Not in a mo... *now*' Nigel shouted.

The receptionist looked up with a worried expression and gently took the telephone piece from Nigel's hand.

'Thank you' she said 'you may sit over there gentlemen' referring to a rather large red leather sofa.

Othman and Nigel sat down and waited for the heavy weight monster to arrive. They weren't disappointed. After only a few seconds this giant of a man burst through the swing doors. He was in his best suit and wore a striped tie. He looked the part apart from the dragon tattoo displayed on what could be seen of his thick neck; the earrings dangling from his left ear; the broken nose and the scar which ran down the left side of his face. His hair was cut very short and he'd obviously decided to give shaving a miss that morning. On the plus side, his suit was sharp, his black shoes clean and his shirt gleaming white. To finish the picture (of this Ronnie Kray look alike) he wore a ring on every finger.

'Where can we talk Grant?' asked Othman.

'In here' said Grant pointing to a door which led to a private conference room.

'Let's cut to the chase Grant' said Othman 'do you know Luke Masterson?'

'I knew him – the poor bastard's dead. It's in the papers.'

'Did he owe you money?'

'No comment.'

'Where were you around 11 to 11.30 pm on 5th August'?

'Having a shag with my missus.'

'That was a very quick response. How can you recall what happened on 5th August just like that. Most normal people would have to think about it?'

'You haven't met my missus.'

'You're going to have to prove your whereabouts Grant.'

' No problem. I've got plenty of witnesses'

'Witnesses? I thought you were with your wife at this time. Were there others in your bed?'

'Of course not. I meant I could provide witnesses for the whole day. I can account for all my movements on that day officer and they don't include Raynes Park.'

'Who mentioned anything about Raynes Park?'

'Cos that's where Luke lives. Everybody in the Exchange knows that.'

'Did you phone June Masterson around 11 pm on 5th August telling her that you were a copper and that her husband had just been killed?'

'Of course not. As I said, I was with my wife. Why would I be phoning Luke's missus – I don't even know her.'

'Let me put this to you smartarse' said Othman 'we know you're part of a drugs ring – we caught you red-handed recently, as you well know, but somehow you got yourself released, probably using a bent solicitor. Anyway, that doesn't matter now. Luke Masterson was also involved in the same racket. You and him were good mates. You went drinking with each other. You worked in the same building. You sold him drugs and he sold them on. Trouble was he began taking too many for himself and failed to get a return. Consequently he couldn't pay you what he owed. You probably threatened him but he still didn't cough up. You need your money. He was becoming a liability. He had to go. You either killed him or you got someone to do it. It's obvious. You had the greatest motive of all – money, your money. Do yourself a favour Grant and tell me this is all true.'

'None of its true. Me and Luke were good buddies. Why would I kill him?'

'He owed you.'

'No he didn't. As I said, we were good buddies.'

'Do you know how he was murdered?'

'Of course I don't.'

'He got a smack on the head with, probably, an iron bar and was stabbed in the back with a large knife. We think there were two of you.'

'Not me mate. You've got the wrong person. I know nothing about any of this.'

'You say you weren't at the scene of the crime. Where were you?'

'I told you – with the missus.'

'What's her number. We'll phone her now.'

Grant gave Othman her number. He tried to call her. She was either out or not answering.

'Give us your address and number Mr O'Malley. We will be meeting with you again, I can assure you.'

'Bollocks' said Grant 'you're just trying to put the frighteners on me. I've got nothing to hide. I'm sorry Luke is dead, he was a nice guy – but I didn't do it.

I'm not into anything as heavy as murder – that's not my style. You'll have to look elsewhere.'

'Oh we will O'Malley' piped up Nigel 'but we start with you as you have a clear motive.'

'So you say officer. Can I go now. I'm going to miss my train.'

'You can go, but we'll be back Grant.'

'Oooooh can't wait gentlemen. Goodbye.'

Grant got up and walked out of the room leaving Othman and Nigel to ponder over the situation.

'Well Othman, what do you think?'

'I don't know, need to do some more digging. He's bound to get people to vouch for him. But he'll make a mistake – you see. He may not have killed Luke Masterson but I bet he knows who did.'

CHAPTER SEVENTEEN

Jon Smithson was a hatchet man. He was an old friend of Grant O'Malley and had carried out many assignments on his behalf. These mostly included roughing up customers who'd failed to make payments to the 'big boss'. On this occasion, he'd been tasked by O'Malley to hurt Luke Masterson and this he attempted to do some time ago, certainly before 5th August, the date of Luke's death. The chain of events were as follows:

As agreed they met at Raynes Park Station and Grant had pointed Luke out to him. They were all under cover of course and this included his partner in crime, Clive. They were to follow Luke to his home and wait for him to reappear the next morning. The plan was to bundle him into their car, drive off to a bit of wasteland and then beat him up unless he came forth with the money. Of course, they knew he wouldn't have the cash on him, but they were prepared to listen to what he had to say about alternative pay arrangements. As it turned out, Luke put up a pretty good fight and, apart from not paying them a penny, laid them out in the middle of some derelict building site in the middle of nowhere and drove their car away! He subsequently dumped the car and made his way to work in the normal way. That evening he made no mention of this incident to his wife, June – he preferred to keep her in blissful ignorance at all times.

What they didn't know, of course, was that one Andrew Garnett had been observing them from the moment they'd arrived at Raynes Park to the moment they'd been laid out on the wasteland. When he saw that they were well and truly beaten, he offered them a lift to the nearest underground station. He took their names and numbers and gave them his card. He told them he would contact them soon as he had a special job for them which was worth a lot of money.

Since establishing his wife was having an affair with Luke, Andrew had been tracking him down and recording his movements – from the time he left the office to the time he arrived home. This demanded a lot of surveillance but Andrew had the time and inclination and was set on taking revenge on his wife's lover. He would deal with Jess in some other way. He hadn't become a successful businessman – with detached property, two cars, two kids and a sexy wife – for nothing and, at the pinnacle of his career, wasn't going to allow some upstart ruin his life without exacting the appropriate punishment. He thought about Shakespeare's play *The Merchant of Venice,* and Shylock's famous speech:

> *'If you prick us do we not bleed? If you tickle us do we not laugh? If you poison us do we not die? And if you wrong us shall we not revenge?*

Yes, revenge would be sweet.

He'd also found out that he wasn't the only one tracking Luke's movements. One Martin Parks had also been keeping a watchful eye and had noticed Luke being bundled into a car. Parks decided to follow them and witnessed the same event as Andrew had. Subsequently the two of them struck up a partnership – both agreeing that something had to be done about Masterson.

It transpired, as we know, that Luke subsequently died.

CHAPTER EIGHTEEN

At the station Othman called a meeting of the whole team assigned to the Luke Masterson murder case. I t was, in all probability, an act of murder. The forensics had determined the time and cause of death and suggested, taking into account the positions, angles and extent of the wounds, that there had been two perpetrators, probably male, and probably of average height. The officers came in one by one and to his surprise Lucy made an entrance. They eyed each other without saying a word. No one Knew they were an 'item' and Othman wanted to keep it that way.

'Okay guys, listen up. We've now established we've got a murder on our hands and, in all probability, there were two involved. Let me summarise what we've got. We know the date, time and place of the murder, and the victim's name – Luke Masterson. We know that he was having an affair with one Jessica Garnett. We know that Luke asked her for money because he owed a Grant O'Malley about 20K. O'Malley is known to us as he was recently caught receiving illegal drugs. He hasn't commented on whether Luke owed him money but denies any involvement in his killing. Grant O'Malley had a motive so he is our number one suspect.'

'But you said there were two of them boss.'

'I did. I'm not saying that O'Malley was necessarily on the scene, but he may have been; what I'm saying is that he had a motive to get rid of Masterson and, therefore, was involved in some way. He may have got a couple of his friends to do his dirty business – we need to find out.'

Othman turned to Joe Palmer and Lucy Deekin, two senior officers on the beat, and told them to keep an eye on O'Malley – to track his movements; to interview his work colleagues and to see what he gets up to when he leaves work.

'Right, the other suspect is Martin Parks. He's our prime witness but when we spoke to him his partner was decidedly hesitant about her relationship with Luke Masterson. We suspect that she had an affair with him, Parks found out and arranged for his murder. Like O'Malley, I doubt whether he carried out the murder, although I suspect he was an accessory. He's got no previous but there's something about him that makes me suspicious. So... he's number two suspect. Parks and his missus are abroad at the moment but when they come back I want you Joe and Lucy to make another visit.'

'Right boss.' Said Joe. 'But what about the other suspects?'

'You mean Andrew Garnett?'

'Yes, and June Masterson.'

'let's take Garnett first. Yes he had a motive. He knew about his wife's affair with Luke and could have arranged for his killing. However, it's unlikely. He's not like O'Malley or Parks. He's a respectable, quiet mannered man with a good job living in one of the most prestigious areas of Wimbledon. Why would he risk giving it all up just because his wife was having a little fling? In any case, she ended the relationship when she found out that Luke was in trouble – not exactly a faithful lover? No, I think it unlikely, although good point Joe.'

'But with respect boss, what you've just said could be completely irrelevant. Just because he comes over as a quiet mannered man doesn't mean to say he can't arrange a murder. The quiet ones are usually the worst.'

'True Lucy but as I said, it's unlikely.'

'And what about June Masterson?' asked Joe.

'Same thing – very unlikely. By the way she doesn't know that her husband was having an affair with her friend Jessica Garnett. In fact she comes over as the perfect wife, unaware of anything that might be going on. She's not in the least suspicious of her husband's affairs – she doesn't, or should I say, didn't get involved with his work or what he did in his spare time. They had a joint account and he used to give her cash when she needed it. She was quite happy focusing on her career and being the good wife, leaving him to run the accounts. She was horrified when she found out that they were in debt. Had she been involved in any part of this she would not have acted in the way she did. She loved her husband and her grief was very genuine. Let's try to be discreet about this. I don't see the point of telling her that her husband was having an affair with her best mate – it would just be adding salt to the wounds. And another thing, June Masterson is pregnant – why an earth would she want to kill the father of her baby – whether he was having an affair or not?'

'I disagree boss' said Lucy. 'I think we'll have to tell her about his affair so that we can gauge her re-action. She's got to be a suspect because she had a motive. You say she didn't know that her husband was having an affair but how do we know she's not lying? She may have known all along and couldn't bear the thought of betrayal. She therefore arranged for his murder.'

'I've met her Lucy and she just doesn't come over as a person capable of such things –she loved Luke and even if she found out he was having an affair, she's the type of person who would forgive his transgressions.'

'She may be just a very good actress?'

'I doubt it. Besides both June and Andrew were at the party when the crime was committed. They have the perfect alibis?'

'Of course' said Joe 'but that doesn't mean they couldn't be accessories?'

'True, but I just can't see how they could have arranged this murder. They don't move in the kind of circles which would enable contact with underworld contract killers.'

'How do you know?'

'I don't for sure I guess. But what about the fact she's pregnant?'

'She's still a suspect boss whether she's pregnant or not' said Lucy.

'I suppose so.'

'Don't you feel further investigation is justified Oth ? (Lucy forgot about his status). After all, we all know that you and Inspector Francis were at the same party. If you don't formally suspect these two then it could be perceived you're involved in a cover up? We know you're not but it's how things look that matters. I'm sure you're right about the two of them but best to investigate and add them to your list. This is not Cairo boss – it's all about how things are perceived and even if you're not protecting them, the press, if they get hold of it, would question why they weren't investigated further.'

Othman paused and considered what was being said. In Cairo it was common practice to go on gut feel and not to worry about how the press interpreted the situation. The police represented ultimate authority – not to be questioned. Perhaps over here it was different.

'You're right Lucy – I guess I still haven't made the transition to the ways of thinking in the UK. I see it now of course – should have seen it sooner. I'll tell you what, let's swap roles. You and Joe follow up on Andrew and June. Nigel and I will keep an eye of O'Malley and Parks. That will stave off any accusations of conflict of interest and, more to the point, I think you and Joe will do a better job than us. You've not met them before and may get a better feel for the situation. Right... unless there's anything else, let's get on with our jobs and report back here in two days time. Keep me advised everybody.'

They all left the meeting apart from Nigel.

'I was just about to intervene Oth as you were clearly going down the wrong path.'

'Yeah, I know that now. Stupid me. First rule of the book – don't be fooled by appearances.'

'You got it. Anyway you redeemed yourself and made the right decision in the end. Let's move on.'

CHAPTER NINETEEN

J on Smithson and Clive Joseph were surprised by
Luke Masterson's ability to look after himself in a
fight and vowed that if there were another opportunity they would dispense with fisticuffs and use more
reliable weapons like knives and coshes. As far as
they were aware they had never killed their victims –
that was not their style – but they had maimed a few
and, certainly, had caused many to end up in A&E
with serious injury. This of course all changed when
they encountered Luke for a second time.

Jon was about 40, medium height, well built,
white with several scars and tattoos displayed on
his face. His parents divorced when he was only five
and he ended up in care. He never got on well with

people telling him what to do and found himself in a gang at the age of twelve. The gang operated in Tottenham where he had lived as a child. No one told him what to do in the gang and so he was happy to survive on the streets with the occasional visit to the home when things got intolerable. He fought his way up the ranks and was soon orchestrating petty crimes in North London. He was quickly convicted of theft and, later, grievous bodily harm, and ended up in prison at the age of 17. It was here that he met his mate Clive Joseph, a lean muscular black guy, and they struck up a business relationship. Their first venture while inside was the illegal importation of drugs which brought them into contact with a young Grant O'Malley. The three of them worked together and although Jon and Clive were forever getting caught and ending up in jail, Grant managed to avoid conviction and led a respectable life – or so it seemed. Grant had the brains while Jon and Clive – unfortunate for them – didn't have a brain between them. So they led a life of crime – mainly theft, drug dealing and assault – and were in and out of prison like a pair of yoyos.

By the time they reached their mid thirties they decided that a quieter life was in order so undertook assignments for O'Malley. These ranged from drug collection and delivery to roughing up those customers who didn't pay up. The way it worked was that O'Malley paid them 50% up front with the rest paid on completion of the job. So with the Luke Masterson case they got paid the initial 50% but when O'Malley found out they'd messed up big time (by being beaten up themselves!), he not only refused to pay them the remainder but demanded full repayment, threatening to hand them over to the police for all the misdemeanours the 'boys in blue' didn't know about – due, of course, to the protection O'Malley was able to give them. Jon and Clive reluctantly paid the money back but found themselves out of pocket. However, they were sure other jobs would emerge and weren't worried too much, especially when Andrew Garnett came on the scene and offered them a proposition which, not being the brightest of people, they jumped at with open arms.

This didn't mean of course that O'Malley had forgotten them – far from it. They were useful in many ways and could always be relied upon to turn up. In any case, as far as he could remember, this was the first job they'd bungled so he wasn't going to give up on them at this stage. In any event, he had another job for them which involved a raid on a supplier's home in Chelsea. O'Malley had kept a low profile since his last encounter with the police but he desperately needed the 20K owed by the late Luke Masterson. As this was not going to be forthcoming he needed to search other avenues and a little burglary job in Chelsea might just provide him with what he wanted. Accordingly, he arranged to meet Jon and Clive in the *Blind Beggar* on the Whitechapel Road.

CHAPTER TWENTY

Meanwhile Joe Palmer and Lucy Deekin had arranged to pay a visit to Andrew Garnett in Wimbledon. It was a very clear morning on the day of their appointment and Lucy was in a particularly good mood. She and Othman were definitely hitting it off and they were now talking about moving in together. Despite this, she wasn't going to get carried away and knew that Othman wanted to move slowly. Nevertheless, the fact that they were discussing moving in together gave her a warm feeling inside.

Joe Palmer on the other hand was not in a good mood. He had recently divorced and could now only see his kids once every other weekend. His ex wife was a solicitor so knew all the loopholes and worked these to her advantage. She pleaded that due to the unreliable nature of Joe's job – never knowing when he was going to be called out; never knowing when he'd come home and never knowing whether he'd been killed or injured during the course of his duties – that it would be more beneficial for their children if a more regular regime were agreed upon. Whilst Joe understood this, it didn't make things any easier and he was dead scared that he was going to lose his children for good. This was not her intention, of course, but she was insistent that their lives be centred around her in her house, rather than around him. Her argument was simply that he could not provide a stable environment and, to a degree, she was right. The previous night they had argued on the phone about his access and like every argument they had, it always ended up with him losing it and hanging up the phone – hence the bad mood this morning.

They drove into the forecourt and Lucy could sense that Andrew was looking out his window behind the curtains. As they approached the front door Andrew opened it and greeted them;

'Ah ha, two new policemen – what a pleasure. Do come in.'

'Do you want us to take our shoes off' asked Joe noticing the cream hall carpet which looked very expensive.

'Don't bother with that, please follow me into the kitchen. Now, tea or coffee?'

They both declined

'Right take a seat. Make yourselves comfortable. You know I've already told your colleagues all I know, so what else is there?'

'We just want to ask one or two further questions Mr Garnett. It won't take long' said Lucy.

'Fine. Fire ahead.'

'When did you first find out that your wife was having an affair?'

'As I told your colleagues, it was some months ago.'

'How did you find out?'

'I became suspicious of her movements. She was always flitting about after she'd completed her household chores. She had a set of friends in the village which she met quite often but then there were other times when she just took off.'

'But how do you know this, you're at work.'

'Not all the time. Besides, I work a lot from home nowadays so I get a feel for what's going on.'

'You say you were suspicious. What were you suspicious about?'

'Look officer, my wife is a very attractive and flirtatious woman. She gets bored when she's not hoovering or clearing up the kitchen. She's got that disease, what's it called? ... yes I know OCD. She's got

OCD and has to check on everything from measuring the blades of grass to scrubbing the oven until she can see her face in the reflection. She denies this of course, saying that she just likes everything in order but her ideas on order are totally different from mine and most other normal people.'

'But tell us when you first discovered that she was having an affair.'

'Well, as I've said, after the hoovering she goes out – sometimes to the gym, sometimes to her coffee meetings and sometimes – who knows? On a whim I decided to follow her. She went to a hotel in Sutton and I saw her meet up with a rather good looking young man. They went into the hotel and came out about one hour later. They did this several times. I started taking photographs – I can show you if you wish?'

'That won't be necessary. Are you still together?'

'Not at the moment. She's taken the kids to her mothers. There needs to be a big cooling off period. To be honest, I don't know whether we shall get back together again.'

'We assume that she admitted to the affair?'

'She tried to fob me off, but when I showed her the photographs she capitulated.'

'How did you feel when you discovered she was having an affair?'

'I felt damned angry. I felt angry with her and angry with him. I later found out that he was the husband of June, a rather nice lady who was part of Jess's coffee set. That made me more angry as she was cheating on both me and her so called friend.'

'Did you have anything to do with Luke Masterson's murder Mr Garnett? asked Joe.

'Certainly not, why an earth would you ask that?'

'Well you had a motive – your wife was having an affair with a good looking young man – your words. You've also told us that you were angry with him. Were you angry enough to want to hurt him Mr Garnett?'

'Of course not. Yes I was angry but not angry enough to want to kill him.'

'Did you think about revenge?'

'No'

'Did you ever follow him?'

'Why would I do that?'

'To find out where he lives so that you could arrange for someone to kill him.'

'That's utter nonsense.'

'Is it? We're not saying that you physically killed him. We think that is unlikely. Besides you were at the party when it happened. But you could have arranged for someone else to do the dirty work?'

'I don't move around in those sort of circles. Who an earth could I ask to carry out a murder?'

'You tell us Mr Garnett. The angry jealous husband might do anything to exact revenge on his wife's lover.'

'Well I didn't arrange or do anything. Sure I was angry, sure I was upset, but I was never involved in his murder – that's the truth.'

'Okay Mr Garnett, thanks for your time. We will see ourselves out. Don't leave the country until our investigations are complete. We may have to speak to you again. Good bye sir.'

Lucy and Joe got into their car and left the fore-court. As they went past the gates Lucy turned round and noticed Garnett peering out the window behind the curtains again.

'What do you think Joe?'

'I'm not sure. He's acting suspiciously but I'm not convinced that he knows anything. The feeling I've got is that he was not very close to his wife. The ways he goes on about her 'disease' and the way she carries on generally didn't give me much confidence that they had a happy marriage. Maybe I'm a bit cynical about relationships at the moment as I've just gone through a divorce as you know.'

'Haven't we all? But what point are you making?'

'Well, if they didn't have a happy marriage why would he care about her indiscretions? Certainly the motive wouldn't be so strong – why would he want to murder his wife's lover if he didn't care about his wife in the first place? – I'd say murder in those circumstances was a bit extreme.'

'Good point Joe. Let's see what June has to say for herself.'

The drive to June's house didn't take long and they soon found themselves looking for a parking space in a pleasant tree-lined road. June's house was detached and enclosed within railings which were tastefully mounted on a small wall running round the forecourt. There was no room for cars in this area so Lucy had to drive past the house to continue her search for a suitable slot. They eventually found one and, after a few attempts, managed to park the car in what was a very tight space. As they left the car it started to pour. They both put newspapers over their heads and ran towards June's house. Thankfully the front gates were open and they managed to reach the comforting shelter provided by a porch which was supported by two neo-classical pillars, without getting too wet. Joe rang the bell and a haggard looking woman opened the door.

'Hello' June said in a timid voice.

'Hi Mrs Masterson, may we come in? We want to talk to you about you late husband. This is officer Palmer and I'm officer Deekin.'

'Oh, you'd better come in. I've already told the police all I know.'

'We know that Mrs Masterson, but we have a few further questions to ask you.'

They were led into the lounge which looked remarkably sparse. There was a long sofa running alongside a wall which faced a coffee table which was covered with letters, bills and statements. Joe and Lucy sat down. June sat in an armchair with her elbows perched on her knees with her face cupped in her hands, looking intently into nothingness and presenting as a gaunt down trodden victim of circumstance.

'Do you want tea, coffee or a cold drink?' she eventually asked.

'No Mrs Masterson, we don't intend staying long because, as you've said, you've told our colleagues everything you know.'

'That's right, so what else did you want to know?'

'Well' Lucy said 'we're sorry to be blunt, but did you know your husband was having an affair?'

'What?'

'Did you know your husband was having an affair?'

'Of course he wasn't. Look I'm pregnant with his baby. We were in love. There was no way he was having an affair. Why an earth would you ask that?'

'I'm afraid it's true. He was having an affair with Jessica Garnett. I think you know who she is?'

'I don't believe you. Is this some kind of joke? Are you trying to trick me in some way? Luke wasn't like that. He liked to have a drink with his mates but he would never cheat on me.'

'Look Mrs Masterson, Jessica Garnett has admitted to her husband that she had an affair with your husband and the only reason she stopped was because he wanted money from her.'

'I don't believe you. As you can see we lived a good life. You're telling me lies. I don't understand.'

June began to well up and reached for some tissues on the coffee table. She started to sob and Joe offered to fetch some water. June declined but continued to cry. There was a pause.

'Look Mrs Masterson, I know this is hard for you and I apologise for my bluntness, but you have to know the truth.'

'Do I?' she sobbed.

'Look, Jessica's husband became suspicious. He followed his wife and found her meeting up with your husband at various hotels. He also found them kissing on Wimbledon Common.'

'What nonsense.'

'He has the photos to prove it. In any case she has admitted it. Do you know anything about this affair Mrs Masterson?'

'Of course I don't.'

'Well, was your husband always home on time? Did he ever leave you during the week or over the weekends?'

'Well of course he did. He would go out with his mates, as I've said. Sometimes he wouldn't get in till late. Sometimes he played golf. He was away quite a bit, but I trusted him. What you're saying is ridiculous.'

'I'm afraid it's not. In fact the situation gets worse I'm afraid. Your late husband was involved in drugs. He owed a so called friend – Grant O'Malley 20K. He couldn't pay up because he was broke. Do you know what your financial position is Mrs Masterson?'

June sat up and repositioned herself in the armchair. She looked out the window with a sigh of resignation. Her demeanour changed. She stopped sobbing but looked as though her world had just completely fallen apart. She got up and walked towards the desk where the statements were kept. She opened a drawer and took out a bunch of papers and brought them back to her armchair.

'We were in debt by some 6K' she said gloomily. 'Luke never involved me with financial matters and I was quite happy not to be involved. I never knew he was involved in drugs. I'm devastated. I don't know what to say.'

'When Jessica found out he was into drugs and was asked to bail him out, she quickly terminated the relationship and never saw him again. If it's any consolation, in our experience, these kinds of relationships never last. They're never based on love. I'm sure Luke loved you June but, like a lot of men, Luke wanted to see whether he was still attractive to other women.'

'That's no consolation at all. I've been deceived all this time and now he's dead.'

'Did you know any of the circumstances leading up to his death?'

'Of course not. Besides, I was at a party when he was killed.'

'Let's put this another way June. We have to establish the suspects. These are people who had a motive to kill your husband.'

'You mean like Grant O'Malley?'

'Exactly. But there are other people who had a motive.'

'Like who?'

'Well, there's Andrew Garnett. He established that his wife was having an affair with your husband. He had a motive. And then there's you – you had a motive because your husband was having an affair with Jessica, your friend.'

'But I didn't know he was having an affair.'

'But say if you did? You would then have a motive.'

'But I didn't.

'But you may be lying. Andrew may have told you and you and he arranged for his killing?'

'That's utter nonsense. Andrew never told me anything. I hardly know him in any case. Do you think that I, a biology lecturer, would be capable of such an act? Firstly I didn't know Luke was having an affair – and I still find that hard to believe, secondly, we were in love and, whether he had an affair or not, I would have stood by him – I certainly wouldn't have killed him, and thirdly, I was at the party when the killing took place.' There was a pause. 'In any case even if I did know about the affair (which I didn't), and even if I did want to arrange to kill him (which I didn't) then how would I go about finding a person who would be willing to do that? I just don't move in those sort of circles.'

'That's funny what you just said. Andrew Garnett said exactly the same thing.'

'What's that?'

'You said that you don't move in those sort of circles. That's exactly what Andrew said. You're not in this together are you Mrs Masterson? Have you had a chance to speak to him so you can get your stories right? It's known as collusion.'

'Of course not – you're going into the realms of fantasy officer. There's been no collusion. As I've said, I hardly know the man. Do you really think that someone like me would involve myself in the criminal underground? I wouldn't know where to start.'

'Maybe, maybe not, but we have to investigate every avenue Mrs Masterson.'

'I know you do and I understand that. But you must believe me, I didn't know he was having an affair and I didn't arrange to kill him. This all sounds so incredible. I don't believe I'm saying this.'

'Okay June, we understand what you're saying. There is another suspect I'm afraid.'

'Who's that?'

'Your neighbour – Martin Parks across the road.'

'But he saw the killers get away. He's your chief witness.'

'We know that. But I have to tell you that his partner may have had an affair with Luke. Parks found out and now he's a suspect.'

'This is getting too surreal.'

'Your late husband was a very handsome man by all accounts. He was a successful businessman until recently and obviously had an eye for the opposite sex. It is not beyond the realms of imagination that he had a little fling with your neighbour and then got found out?'

'I think I've had enough of all this officer. It's all conjecture. There's no proof of anything. Besides, why would Martin declare himself as a witness when he was behind the killing?'

'May be to put us off his scent – a distraction so that we would eliminate him from our enquiries – who knows? All I'm saying is that there are currently four suspects in this case – O'Malley, Parks, Andrew and yourself.'

'But I think you're going to need a bit more evidence before you can start arresting people – you've got nothing but suspects. And you can count me out because I'm pregnant with Luke's baby – I loved him and would never have hurt him. I don't care how many affairs he had – as long as he came home to me, I wouldn't have minded. The thought of me arranging for his murder is unthinkable. It just wouldn't have happened no matter how many lovers he had. I'll tell you for the last time – I didn't know about his affairs and I certainly didn't arrange for his murder. Now I need some rest. Can you go now please. I really want to be alone.'

'Of course Mrs Masterson. We'll see our own way out. Goodbye for now.'

The two of them made their way back to the car. The rain had stopped.

'What do you think Joe?'

'I don't know. She seems an unlikely suspect. On the other hand she kept repeating that she didn't know anything about the affair or that she didn't arrange to murder her husband. Sometimes, when people are so defensive, they're usually hiding something.'

'True, but it all comes down to whether we believe her or not.'

'In fairness, she makes some good points, although I have to say, she does come over as a totally naive innocent.'

'That's what I thought. She may be a quiet academic, but no one is that naive are they?'

''There's nowt as queer as folk'' Lucy. She may be naive but she puts on a good act – whether she's naive or not.'

'Right, I wonder how Othman is getting on?'

CHAPTER TWENTY-ONE

Othman and Nigel waited in their car outside the building in which O'Malley worked. They both sipped their coffees and exchanged theories on who was behind Luke's murder. Just as they were getting deep into conversation, O'Malley emerged from the front entrance. He stopped by the steps, looked both ways and made his way the nearest pub. They waited. After about ten minutes Othman decided to enter the pub and find out what was going on. Just as he was about to open the front door to the pub he noticed O'Malley finishing his drink and turning round to make for the exit. Othman quickly retreated back to the car. O'Malley came out of the pub and headed towards the underground.

'I'm going to follow him Nigel. You can make your way back to the station and I'll keep you posted.'

'it's your call Oth. Don't do anything stupid.'

'Wouldn't dream of it. See you later.'

Nigel drove off and Othman followed O'Malley to the Bank keeping a reasonable distance but ensuring he was in sight. The crowds were gathering in the underground as commuters lined up to take their turn at the ticket barriers. O'Malley was difficult to miss and Othman had no problem in tracking him down until they reached the platform headed for the East End of London. The train whistled in and both men managed to squeeze past the commuters until they stood on the safety line, preparing themselves for the mad rush to find a space. They were at either end of the carriage but Othman could make out the huge frame of O'Malley and was able to check whether he was going to stay or get off at any particular station. He got off at Mile End and made his way to the *Blind Beggar*. Othman followed having advised Nigel his whereabouts. On entering the pub O'Malley saw his two partners in crime – Jon and Clive – propping up the bar.

'How long have you been here?' he asked.

'About an hour' said Jon 'what're you drinking?'

'I don't believe it – you're not going to buy a round?'

'Only one. You got all the money Grant so the rest is down to you.'

'Okay. Let's find a table.'

The three men managed to find a small table in a far corner and took several gulps of beer.

'Right you two 'erberts', I ain't got much time.'

'What's the crack?' asked Clive.

'Got a job down in Chelsea. A supplier. Very rich geezer. Got a tip off from an old mate of mine.'

'Tip off?'

'Yeah. The geezer whose name is of no consequence will be out tomorrow night from about 7.30 pm to the early hours.'

'How do you know?'

'Because my mate will be entertaining him. They go back a long way although there's no loyalty.'

'So what?'

'I want you two to break in and steal his diamond necklaces.'

'Where are they kept?'

'Where do you think Clive – displayed on the dining room table?'

'You know what I mean boss.'

'They're in a safe in the cellar ... believe it or not I've got the code.'

'How did you get that?'

'Don't ask. My mate reckons there's about 50k's worth. That means 30k for me and 20K for you two. Are you up for it me lovelies?'

'What's the catch?'

'There's no catch. The only thing you've got to figure out is how to break in and how to get out without being noticed... should be easy, even for a couple of bunglers like you.'

'Nothing's easy anymore' said Jon.

'Bullshit. Are you up for it or not?'

'Of course we are.'

'Right here's the address. Keep me posted. And no f..k ups.' There was a pause 'Now, tell me about the other night when you were supposed to be extracting money from the late Luke Masterson. What went wrong?'

'We tracked him down as you told us but he could handle himself.'

'And you can't... you pair of nancies.'

'He drove off with our car, the bastard. Then this guy offered to drive us to the underground. He'd been watching us the whole time. He told us he wanted Masterson out the way cos he was carrying on with his wife.'

'And what did you say?'

'We told him we don't do killing.'

'And?'

'Well to cut a long story short, he offered us 60K and told us he would provide an old untraceable van.'

'For what?'

'For our getaway.'

'So you two are now *Bonny and Clyde*?'

'It was an offer we couldn't refuse. Besides we wanted to teach that bastard a lesson.'

'So you killed him?'

'We didn't mean to. We just wanted to hurt him. We figured we could get the rest of our money from this geezer whether we killed him or not.'

'What was his name?'

'Andrew something... he was a bit posh and wimpish. We didn't think we'd have any problem in getting what was due. We would have done him over otherwise.'

'So did you get the money?'

'We got 30K from him.'

'What about the rest?'

'We don't know where that came from. It wasn't from him. We were told to pick up an envelope from some builder in Raynes Park.'

'And did you?'

'Yeah, though we didn't see him. We just knocked on the door and a hand came round with an envelope. We were then told to piss off, which we did.'

'So you've been paid in full?'

'You bet. You're the only person we've told so don't go blabbing to the police.'

'What about this Andrew geezer and the builder?'

'They obviously wanted Masterson out the way and were willing to pay a couple of thugs like us to do the dirty business. Having said that, we had no intention of killing him. As I said we would have got our money one way or the other.'

'Right you too. Do this job tomorrow and I'll keep my mouth shut. Got it?'

'How do we know you're not going to grass?'

'Because we're a team... honour among thieves and all that fine stuff. However, We'll talk about that later. For now get this Chelsea job done.'

They spent the next couple of minutes supping their beers and were then interrupted by a stranger:

'Good evening gentlemen. May I have a chat?' Othman asked just as they were about to move away from their table.

'Who are you?' Clive asked.

'Can't you tell Clive... it's the filth. You can smell him a mile away.'

Before anybody knew what had happened Othman grabbed Jon's arm and shot it up his back causing him to wail like a baby.

'Now let's all sit down and play nice' said Othman 'Where I come from, when you speak like that to a law enforcement officer you're thrown in the clink.'

'But this ain't Africa mate and you've just committed assault' said Jon.

'Insulting a police officer is provocation enough dickhead.' There was a short pause. 'Now, I know your boss here – a Mr Grant O'Malley who's been questioned before on the murder of one Luke Masterson. Do you know anything about this boys?'

'As I've already told you officer' said O'Malley 'it's got nothing to do with me and nothing to do with my colleagues here.'

'And who are your colleagues Mr O'Malley. Can they speak for themselves or are they as thick as they look?'

'We know nothing about any murder mate' said Jon 'We're just having a quiet drink with our old buddy. We ain't breaking no law and you can't touch us.'

'Maybe, maybe not, but the mere fact you're talking to this man (pointing to O'Malley) makes me very suspicious. What are your connections?'

'We have many but none of them are any of your business. As my colleague has just said drinking in pubs is not prohibited so either state what you want to state or just leave us alone.'

'Okay I want your names and addresses.'

'My name's Micky Mouse' said Jon.

'And my name is Donald Duck' said Clive.

'And my name is Inspector Francis' said Nigel as he made his entrance followed by two police officers. 'And you lot are wanted for questioning down at the station. Your carriage awaits you gentlemen so get up and accompany these two fine young constables to the van outside.'

While driving back to the station Nigel informed Othman that Jon Smithson and Clive Joseph were known to the police as petty, but sometimes violent criminals, with plenty of previous.

During the subsequent interviews down at the station, all three of them denied everything and provided the names of alibis who could vouch for their movements on the night of the murder. These people were quickly gathered up and interviewed. They all corroborated their colleague's stories.

The police had come to a dead end; no finger prints, no murder weapons, no van ... with four or even six suspects who either had alibis or, in the case of Andrew Garnett and June Masterson, had a mass of evidence, including that provided unwittingly by Othman and Nigel, which showed they couldn't possibly have been at the site of the murder when it was committed.

Both Othman and Nigel were summoned to a meeting by Superintendent Wilkins.

CHAPTER TWENTY-TWO

Superintendent Sarah Wilkins was in her fifties, hardnosed - having competed with the opposite sex for most of her professional life – and, above everything else, fair and principled. She didn't like time wasters, bull shitters or egocentric upstarts. She was not the most attractive of women – with her stern face and hair swept back from her forehead and tied in a bun at the back (which had the effect of exaggerating the size of her rather large nose) – but her figure was lean and her legs were long which gave her a presence which was at best intimidating and at worst downright scary! Officers did not want to get on the wrong side of Superintendent Sarah Wilkins.

She was brought up in Enfield, went to Hendon Training College to complete her police training and made her way up the ranks by sheer hard work, study and tenacity. She could look after herself physically having achieved black belt status in both Judo and Karate, and was not afraid of diving in when the going got tough on the streets.

A formidable Superintendent but devoted wife and mother. Her husband was a corporate lawyer and her two children were both attending university. With regard to the Luke Masterson case this, for some reason, had been kept away from her as the Assistant Chief had personally allocated investigations to Inspector Othman for reasons she was not quite sure. Anyway, he had delegated the case to her as he had other things to contend with, like an extended holiday, and, after reading the reports, had concluded that progress had been remarkably slow. She read the reports a second time and looked out of her office window hoping for some inspiration. Instead, she became furious!

'Sit down gentlemen. This case is now under my watch and to say that I'm concerned would be an understatement.'

'Why ma'am?' asked Nigel.

'You don't know Inspector? It's bloody obvious.'

'Please explain.'

'You two were at the same party when June Masterson's husband was killed were you not?'

'Yes.'

'Well you two are the best alibis in this case. You can't go investigating a case when you have special connections with two of the suspects! That's unethical, unfair and wrong at every level.'

'But we didn't have special connections with these two suspects ma'am - we didn't know them from Adam.'

'That may be so, but it's all about how things *appear* Inspector Othman. Also how do I or anybody else for that matter know for sure that you two don't have connections with the suspects – you were at the same bloody party sitting round the same bloody table dressed up as two bloody idiots drinking the same bloody wine – For all I know you may have been engaged in the same bloody party games?'

'As it happens ma'am I stopped one of the games because it was getting too serious' said Othman.

Nigel looked at Othman as if to say – *you're now in it right up to your neck*!

'Is that so Inspector Othman. Have you heard the expression 'digging your own grave?'

'As a matter of fact, I have ma'am.'

'Well you've not only dug it but you're now lying in it with me shovelling in as much dirt as I can muster. Do you get my meaning Inspector?'

'Of course ma'am but the bottom line is this. The Assistant gave me this case because of my objectivity and whether we attended the party or not, it has made no difference to the outcome. We are where we are.'

'That may be so but as I said before, it's all a matter of perception and appearance. Had you captured the villains we may not have been talking about this subject. But since you haven't, and as time moves on, It looks more and more difficult for you Inspector and, to a lesser degree you Mr Francis, to maintain any kind of objectivity or, indeed, credibility in this case. That's where I'm coming from.'

'What do you suggest ma'am?'

'You've got one week. If you haven't come up with anything positive by then, both of you will be removed from the case. Have you got that gentlemen?'

'We certainly have.'

'Now sort this out as quickly as possible before it becomes a total embarrassment for the station.'

The two of them got up from their chairs and scurried out like two naughty children. They got to the door:

'Oh, and another thing, did you ever find out who made the call to June Masterson in the first place? He evidently had an Irish accent.'

'Dead end ma'am. We couldn't track down the caller. Someone is obviously lying. O'Malley has denied making the call and none of the others are Irish.'

'So what? They may have put on an Irish accent. Get out of my office and sort this case out.'

They exited the office with some pace.

'What's the plan Othman?'

'A couple of pints in the *Spotted Horse.*'

'Good idea.'

CHAPTER TWENTY-THREE

J essica Garnett had spent the last couple of weeks with her mother and was miserable. She had confessed to Andrew, apologised profusely, demonstrated genuine remorse and had asked him for another chance. The fact of the matter was that deep down she loved him and he was the father of her children. She'd reflected on her situation and was determined to be a good wife from now on. She would convince him over time provided they could get back together again that she had changed. She had learnt her lesson and wasn't getting any younger – the days of affairs, coffee mornings and dinner parties were well and truly over. She must now be the dutiful wife. She had so much to lose – after all Andrew was the bread winner and without his income her life wouldn't be the same. No, she must make amends – settle down in a traditional marriage and then, perhaps, work out where she wanted to be when the kids left home. Besides, her mother was getting on her nerves and she doubted whether she could stay in her house any longer. Her father didn't say a word and just sat in the lounge reading a newspaper. It was like being in a residential nursing home and Jess had had enough. She phoned Andrew:

'Don't hang up, I want to discuss things with you in a calm way.'

'Why should I – you cheated on me.'

'I know and I'm sorry. It will never happen again.'

'Not only did you cheat on me but you've treated me as your slave over the years – I was always at your beck and call. I've had enough.'

'I know. I've been reflecting on the past and I've been a bitch to you. I'm sorry. But things will change from now on, I promise you. Please give me one final chance.'

'Okay you'd better come over this afternoon. I'm not making any promises mind you because I think our marriage is over. Come over anyway. I'll see you about 2 pm.'

Andrew got up and headed for the bathroom leaving a rather attractive woman lying naked on his bed. They showered together, got dressed and went down stairs to the kitchen. They spent another couple of hours on the sofa talking about trivia and drinking coffee. At around 1.30 pm the woman left having agreed to meet him the following day in a pub in the city. They said their goodbyes, kissed and went their different ways – she back to her home, he back to his sofa. He was going to pour himself a large whisky.

Jess arrived on time and could immediately tell that Andrew had been on the booze. Normally she'd admonish him for such behaviour, but this time she let it pass thinking that she needed to demonstrate straightaway that she'd changed.

'Come in Jess. Want a drink? I've opened a bottle of Black Label.'

'Not for me Andrew but you go ahead.'

They sat down opposite each other and there followed an awkward silence. Jess decided to commence proceedings:

'Look Andrew, I'm terribly sorry for what I did, but for the sake of the children, if nothing else, let's give our marriage another try – I'm begging you.'

'So you can cheat on me again Jess? No way.'

'I swear to you I won't. As I said I've had enough time to ponder over my behaviour and I've changed. I want to come back.'

'Getting fed up with your mother more like.'

'That's not fair Andrew. I'm begging you for a second chance. If you care for me and the children at all, you will at least grant me that. If I become a bitch again, then throw me out. I will have deserved it.'

Andrew considered his position. There was another awkward silence. He wasn't about to make it easy for Jess.

'When I found out you were having an affair I was broken hearted. I became suspicious at first and then I started tracking you down. I can't tell you how hurt I was when I discovered you were with that Luke Masterson.'

'I know, it must have been terrible for you. I let you down.'

'You did. I thought we had a stable marriage with two lovely kids. Okay you were difficult with your obsessive behaviours and your bitchiness, but I forgave you – I was prepared to live with all that.'

'I know, I know. How many times do you want me to apologise?'

'I couldn't stand the man you were with. He was tall, handsome and everything I wasn't.'

'Yes, but I didn't love him. It was purely physical. He was a loser. I had no feelings for him at all.'

'Yes but what about your feelings for his wife June? How do you think she feels – or do you care?'

'Does she know?'

'I expect so. The police would have to tell her to gauge her reaction. She's a suspect as well as myself.'

'Oh my God, I've done so much damage. What do I do now?'

'It's more than that. I was so upset with Masterson. How could he have an affair with my wife – the mother of my children. I was incensed. I therefore tracked his movements in the same way I tracked yours.'

'So did you have anything to do with his murder?'

'Of course not – I couldn't do anything like that. You must know me by now. I'm as gentle as you are obnoxious.'

'But I've learnt my lesson. I'm not like that anymore.'

'Well, I don't know, time will tell. Anyway, I followed him one evening before his murder and saw two guys bundle him into their car the next morning'

'What, you stayed in the car all night?'

'Yes, you see, the night before, I saw him being followed by two men. They parked outside Luke's house and I guessed that something would happen either that night or the following day. I was proved to be right. Anyway, the next morning I saw Luke come out of his house and get bundled into their car. I then followed them to some wasteland. The three got out and said something to each other. I couldn't hear what they said. But the conversation got heated and the two of them attacked Luke.'

'What did you do?'

'Nothing, I was pleased he was going to get a bloody good hiding. Unfortunately he didn't. Luke obviously knew how to handle himself and within a minute left them lying on the ground – bruised and cut I suspect. He then got into their car and drove off.'

'What happened next?'

'I gave them a lift to the station.'

'Why?'

'I don't know. I guess I thought they could help me teach Masterson a lesson. I gave them my card. Next thing I know Luke gets killed.'

'Do you think it was the same two guys who tried to beat him up?'

'Possibly, I don't know. Anyway, put it this way, when I found out that Luke had been murdered I wasn't exactly crying in my tea.'

'Have you told the police about this?'

'Of course not, and nor should you if you want to have a second chance with me.'

'But withholding information like this is not right.'

'Who are you to talk about what's right Jess – you haven't exactly been squeaky clean yourself?'

'That's not the point. Two wrongs don't make a right.'

'Look Jess. I'll be plain, keep you big mouth shut otherwise they'll be no 'we'.'

'Are we going to get back together or not?'

'I need time to think. I thought it was all over. This is the first time you've made contact with me. Let me mull it over in my head.'

'What's there to mull over Andrew – you are either going to give me a chance or not.' Jess's manner changed – she became more feisty. With this new disclosure she was becoming suspicious of Andrew's involvement. There was a limit to her begging. She took on a more sterner, more intense look on her face. She fidgeted in the armchair, got up walked around and resumed her position facing him. Andrew detected the old Jess coming back – she looked slightly manic.

'As I said, I need more time.'

'How much time?' Jess asked in a raised voice.

'I don't know.'

'I need the loo.'

'Well, you know where it is.'

Jess made her way to the downstairs loo. She looked at herself in the mirror. She wondered whether it was, after all, all over. Andrew had got himself involved with two villains and hadn't reported this to the police. This could become messy. Say if Andrew did arrange for Luke's murder? Where would their relationship go if he were convicted. That wouldn't suit Jess. On the other hand, he may be telling the truth in which case she must stand by her husband. But he was acting strangely. He wouldn't give her an answer as to whether they could get back together again. She had been totally honest with him – even begged him (which wasn't her style). She was in confusion. She wished he hadn't told her about his surveillance campaign leading ultimately, she thought, to Luke's death. This was not right. This was becoming messy – she didn't do messy.

She went to put her hair brush in her handbag and noticed a tissue on the glass shelf. She picked it up and noticed it had been used –there were lipstick marks everywhere. She smelt it – it wasn't the make she uses. Has Andrew been a naughty boy? She went back to the lounge and saw Andrew take another slug of whisky.

'I found this tissue in the loo and there's a distinct smell of woman in the hallway and indeed, come to think of it, in here. Have you been entertaining Andrew or have you decided to initiate a transgender campaign for yourself?'

'I don't know what you're talking about. I can't smell anything.'

'Well what about this' she said showing him the lipstick stained tissue. 'What's this all about?'

'It's probably yours or perhaps its Olga's –she might have left it there.'

'You can't fool me Andrew. This is not mine and Olga never wears lipstick. Anyway, she would never enter the downstairs loo. She knows that's out of bounds – she's got her own loo.'

'You're talking rubbish Jess, as usual – you haven't changed. You're still the bitch. Don't forget that I'm the victim here. It was you that went off with another man.'

'And it's clear to me that you've gone off with another woman. We're quits now Andrew. We've both sinned so why don't you just admit it so we can all move forward.'

'I'm not admitting anything because I haven't done anything. I think you'd better go now.'

'Too right I'm going to the police and I'm taking this tissue with me.'

Andrew who, by now, was well under the influence of alcohol shouted:

'No you're not' as he grabbed her wrist and twisted it round until she dropped the tissue. He went to pick it up but jess pushed him causing him to lose balance. She then grabbed the tissue and ran to the front door. Andrew regained his composure, moved quickly to the door and was able to catch Jess by the neck before she could do anything else.

'Let go 'she screamed.

'Give me that tissue.'

They struggled. Jess managed to turn round and kneed him in the groin. He doubled over and she was able to open the front door and run towards the car. She got in and locked the doors. She turned the ignition. It wouldn't start. She tried again – still no good. At the same time Andrew came running toward s the car and attempted to open the passenger's door. Thankfully the central locking system had worked. He pounded his fists on the roof and told her to get out. At the third attempt Jess managed to start the engine, put the gears in first and stamped on the accelerator. The car screeched as the tyres spun round forcing the stones beneath to spray across the front of the forecourt. The car nearly hit the side of the wall as it made its exit to the road. But Jess got out unharmed and made her way back to her mother's house. When she arrived she carefully picked the tissue from her handbag, smelt the lipstick again and called Inspector Othman.

━━╪━ ━╪━━

Andrew had to make a quick couple of phone calls. He phoned Jon and Clive first and told them he had a problem and wondered whether they could help him out. He explained that his wife knew about his connections with the two of them and, normally, this would not have caused a problem. However, 'that damned bitch', as he referred to her, had found out about his indiscretions with a certain lady and was going to reveal all to the police. She had to be stopped.

'Just rough her up enough to put her off going to the police. Threaten her, of course, but don't kill her. Just put the frighteners on her. She'll back off I know it, but warn her of the consequences if she doesn't. Do you know what I mean guys?'

'Sure we do' said Jon 'but it will cost you?'

'How much?'

'30K'

'Okay. Go ahead as quick as you like.'

Andrew gave them Jess's mother's address and her mobile number and hung up. He then made another phone call, explained the situation and asked for a contribution towards the bill.

'Not this time Andrew. It's your mess, not mine. You didn't have to disclose the fact that you got involved with Luke's killers – at least I guess they were his killers; and you should have been more careful when clearing up after your girlfriend. I'm surprised Jess's obsession with cleaning hasn't rubbed off on you. Had you been a bit more domesticated you would have checked and cleaned every room that you and her had occupied – including the loo. Sorry Andrew, but you're on your own on this one.'

'Well you better think again cos If I go down, I'm taking you with me.'

'I'll deny everything darling. I wasn't involved. In fact I've got enough on you now to make your life a misery.'

'You wouldn't – we were both in this together. You'd still be implicated.'

'I'll take that chance – goodbye sweetie.'

CHAPTER TWENTY-FOUR

J ess explained the situation to Othman and he told her to stay exactly where she was. Her mother lived in Tooting Bec, not far from the station and near the high street. Othman reckoned he could get down there in thirty minutes and, without further ado, hijacked Nigel's BMW and sped out of the station compound. When he arrived he found nowhere to park so decided to use the *Asda* car park, ensuring he displayed his police identity on the front windscreen. He literally ran to the house, knocked on the door and was greeted by a little old lady in her eighties.

'Suppose you want to see Jessica?' the little old lady asked. 'Do come in.'

Othman found himself in a rather large front room filled with expensive looking antique furniture. The carpets and wallpaper were floral in design and clashed badly. However, Othman could tell that no expense had been spared in the decor and despite the rather eccentric tastes, the room exuded quality. He was asked to sit down in a regency armchair and wait for Jess to finish showering.

'She's always showering that girl – I'm surprised she's got any skin left. You went to the same university I gather?'

'Yes, that's right, many years ago.'

'Ah here she comes – I'll leave you two to it.'

'Hi Jess – you okay?'

'Not really had a big bust up with Andrew.'

'And?'

'To cut a long story short, he told me, as I said on the phone, that he'd been tracking Luke and witnessed an attempt by two thugs to beat him up.'

'Where was this?'

'Somewhere in the Raynes Park area.'

'Anyway, Luke managed to lay them both out, took their car and drove off. Andrew told me that he offered to take the two of them to the nearest underground. When I asked him why, he said he might use them to help him punish Luke – I think those were the words he used. Any way as you know Luke died soon after that incident.'

'Why did he tell you all this?'

'I don't know. I think he thought he had one over me. I went to see him initially to beg forgiveness so I guess he thought that I would keep a secret.'

'So why haven't you.'

'Well I may have done ... I'm not sure. But what swung it for me was this.' Jess showed Othman the tissue.

'That's not my lipstick and it certainly isn't Olga's. That's the lipstick of a girl, I suspect, he's been having an affair with.'

'Well Jess, you can't be sure of that, but it does look suspicious. We can run some tests on this. We might be able to get some DNA. What make is this lipstick?'

'Chanel Number Three.'

'How come you're so certain?'

'I'm an expert in these matters darling. Go and check it out. Boots will stock it.'

'How did your meeting with your husband end?'

'Badly. He wanted that tissue back. He nearly strangled me to get it but I got away. He'd completely lost it Othman and virtually chased me down the road.'

'Okay stay put. I suspect the last thing your husband wanted was for you to go to the police. He certainly acted suspiciously when you discovered the tissue. Who knows, he may have even asked his criminal friends to put the frighteners on you. I'm going to sanction a couple of officers to keep a watch over this house – is that okay with you?'

'A bit dramatic Othman – I'm sure I'm safe here.'

'Best to be cautious Jess. You don't know what your husband may be capable of. By the way, who's looking after the kids?'

'Olga will be looking after them, together with my mother – I don't see a problem there. Andrew may be turning into a psycho but he would never harm his children.'

'I hope you're right. I'm going to get this tissue analysed and pay a visit to your husband. Meanwhile, don't answer the phone, don't go out and await my call. I've got a week to sort this out so you won't have to wait long – hopefully. Oh, and another thing, take a photograph of that bruise forming round your neck. I'm assuming Andrew did that so you need to come with me to the lab.'

'What now?'

'Yes now. When you're finished I'll arrange for you to be escorted back to your mother's house.'

Othman left Jess and the tissue with the lab boys and made his way back to Wimbledon. He thought about involving Nigel and the rest of the team but decided that he would have to do this on his own. He assumed he was being watched closely by MI5 in view of his previous activities, and was now being watched by Superintendent Wilkins to ensure his competence in the job. It was now up to him to do the business and this he would do in his own style ... a few feathers may be ruffled but he would get there in the end.

'Good evening Mr Garnett. May I come in?'

'Ah Inspector Othman – what a pleasure. Come this way.'

Othman sat down on the sofa and Andrew nestled in his armchair.

'Now what can I do for you?'

'I'll get to the point Mr Garnett. Jess came round to see you this afternoon asking for your forgiveness. You disclosed to her that you'd been following Luke Masterson and witnessed him beating up two men. You drove these men to the nearest underground and told them you wanted to take revenge on your wife's lover – or words to that effect. You probably gave them your card and promised you would pay them to do your dirty work. You told Jess to keep quiet about your little story and she probably would have, had it not been for a tissue she found in your loo. That tissue is being analysed as we speak. Now, I know who these two guys are. You see, Luke owed a Grant O'Malley 20K for drugs he hadn't sold on.

Luke didn't cough up so Grant got his two hench-men to rough him up. That's when you came in and witnessed the very opposite of what should have hap-pened. Instead of walking away you got yourself in-volved and paid them to kill Luke Masterson. That's it in a nutshell isn't it Mr Garnett?'

'What utter nonsense Inspector. You know how Jess's imagination runs wild on occasions. She did come round asking for forgiveness and I was pre-pared to forgive her. This story about me track-ing Luke and then offering his assailants money to get rid of him is total rubbish. Jess is fantasising Inspector – you know what she's like. It was when she found the tissue that she went all weird – thinking that I was having an affair. That's what turned her and made her create this ludicrous story. So what if I'm having an affair. Your analysis may prove that it's not my wife's DNA – nor Olga's for that matter – but who cares? It's got nothing to do with Luke's murder.'

'Who are you having an affair with?'

'No one. Again, it's all in her mind. She's not ra-tional. Come to think of it, she's never been rational. I'm glad she's gone Inspector. Look, I'm not having an affair, I haven't been tracking down Luke, I didn't witness any fight and I didn't arrange for Luke's mur-der. You know, despite my motive, I couldn't possibly have killed Luke myself because I was at the same party as your good self. Now, unless there's anything else, I want to watch the 10 o'clock news. Goodbye Inspector Othman.'

'I'm not going yet Mr Garnett. When Jess refused to hand you over the tissue you went berserk and grabbed her neck – she showed me the bruising. Why were you so annoyed with her? What was the importance of that tissue? Why, Mr Garnett did you assault your own wife?'

'Again, all evidence from a mad woman. I didn't assault her in any way. She probably strangled herself – you know how dramatic she can be. It's her word against mine Inspector and unless you have any further evidence, your investigations are going nowhere.'

'We shall see Mr Garnett. But don't think you're off the hook.'

'Why's that?'

'Because I know Jess. She may be many things but she's not a liar. I believe everything she's said. On the other hand I don't believe a word that's come out of your mouth. You may think this is going nowhere, but believe me when I know someone's lying, I don't let go. Don't leave the country Mr Garnett.'

'I don't intend to – I've got nothing to hide.'

'Oh, and another thing. You left your finger prints all over your wife's neck so if she decides to prosecute, you'll be up for assault.'

'You're bluffing Inspector. I didn't harm her in any way. I'll deny everything.'

'That's up to you Mr Garnett but, as I've said before, don't leave the country. Doubtless I'll be seeing you again.'

'I look forward to it Inspector – Goodbye.'

CHAPTER TWENTY-FIVE

That night Jon and Clive met in a pub on the kings Road. They had just received a call from Andrew Garnett advising them that Jess had already made contact with the police and it was too late to do anything about it. All deals were off and they had better keep their heads down as the ' filth were sniffing around' (since meeting Jon and Clive Andrew had become familiar with criminal terminology and rather liked using it!). He told them that he had denied everything and swore blind that he had never followed Luke around or knew anything about them.

Jon and Clive looked at each other and realised the 'noose was tightening.'

'What do we do?' asked Clive.

'We sit tight. We'll do the job in Chelsea as planned and decide what we do with the merchandise.'

'What do you mean?'

'Well, it's all very well for Grant to use us to get his money, but we'll be in the frontline. He'll be in some pub somewhere leaving us to do his dirty work.'

'But that's the way it's always been?'

'I know, and I'm getting fed up with it. Look, we could simply take what we can and make a run for it. We could lie low in Milton Keynes with me mum for a few months.'

'But sorry Jon, your mother doesn't stop moaning – she's a nightmare.'

'I know, but what's the alternative?'

'Suppose so, but Grant will grass on us.'

'So what, that won't go anywhere. He'll tell the filth we killed Masterson and we'll deny it. We've got alibis we can rely on and, besides, the police will think his grassing is a distraction to get him off the hook. Don't forget, he had a motive for killing Masterson. We didn't, we just did the dirty work. They won't have any fingerprints, the van has been burnt to a cinder, no one saw us, so what's the problem? We take the money and run.'

'And of course, Grant doesn't know anything about our Milton Keynes hideaway. Come to think of it, nor does that Garnett fella. We'd be home free?'

'Exactly, now make sure you've got all the codes. I've got the disabling kit cos there's bound to be CCTV and security cameras all over the place. Have you got a shooter?'

'Of course.'

'Good hopefully we won't need it but who knows. I've got me cosh and knife – me trusted friends – so let's make a move.

Meanwhile Grant was sipping a beer in the corner of the same pub. He suspected his boys might take matters into their own hands so, to be on the safe side, he was going to be around when they'd collected the riches from the house.

It was 1 am in the morning and the king's Road was quietening down. There was still a buzz about the place as the first revellers came out of the clubs to look for a cab or to walk aimlessly along the road until they remembered which direction they should take in order to get home. There was a lull in the proceedings until about 4 am when the next batch would surface from the bars, wobble about on the pavements, and then make dubious attempts to take the journey home. The time between was the best time to make a raid on a home which was positioned in a side street off the main road in the Chelsea area.

It was dark and cloudy and only the street lights illuminated the area. There was no visible moon and the stars were certainly not twinkling. Jon and Clive arrived at the front of the house in their old Ford Cortina and parked at the gates. Jon jumped out, pressed the four digits which released the gates and allowed them to park the car at the front door. They spotted the CCTV and security lights and before Clive had turned off the engine, Jon had taken the ladders from the car roof and had de activated both appliances. Meanwhile Clive had unlocked the front door with the keys Grant had given him (it remains a mystery regarding how Grant came by these, but, probably, his friend had secured them on a temporary basis, allowing Grant to make copies – who knows?) broken the internal chain and disarmed the alarm. Time was of the essence - it wouldn't take long before a neighbour was disturbed by the unusual behaviour of two men in black.

They both entered the large hallway and used their torches to light up the area leading to the kitchen. The kitchen was easily identified as it was located at the end of the house at the bottom of the hallway. With gloved hands they tried each door as they made their way down the hall – since they were in the house they saw no problem in 'nosing about' – who knows what they could find. There were three reception rooms, all tastefully decorated and filled with modern furniture. They had no time to ponder the niceties of modern decor and swiftly approached the kitchen room door having assessed the lack of profitable bounty in the other rooms. It was unlocked as anticipated and the two villains entered the room and looked for the door leading to the cellar. Clive tripped over a bucket, the contents of which went sprawling over the floor...

'What are you doing you half wit?'

'I didn't see it' said Clive.

'Well, keep the noise down for Christ sake. Clear up the mess and put the bucket back to where it was. I'm going to unlock the cellar door.'

The door was locked but Jon snapped the lock without too much effort.

'All right, that's done, now follow me and keep quiet – we don't want to wake up the whole bloody neighbourhood.'

They went down the wooden steps to a very murky cellar.

'Shall I turn on the light?' asked Clive.

'Of course not. Keep your torch on.'

The walls were damp and there was rubbish everywhere. The room stank of rotten flesh and both of them covered their faces to avoid the stink.

'Someone must've died down here' said Clive.

'Too right. Let's get what we've come for and make a quick exit.'

Just as Jon had finished his sentence a hoard of rats came from nowhere and darted across the room jumping over their feet as they did so...

'What the f..k' cried Clive as his torch fell from his hand 'let me out – I can't stand rats.' Clive made for the stairs. Jon grabbed him...

'Cool it Clive. They won't hurt you – they've already had their meal.' Jon pointed to a dead dog in the corner of the room. The rats had disembowelled the poor creature and only the tail and ears were left suggesting the remains of a Golden Retriever.

'How the hell did that dog get in here?' asked Clive.

'Probably the owners forgot to let him out. Who knows?' Anyway, we've got a job to do so let's get on with it.'

'At least that explains the stink' said Clive.

The two of them stared at the remains of the dog and Clive shuddered as the last rat took refuge in the shadows of the cellar.

'Can't stand rats' repeated Clive who was now getting on Jon's nerves.

'I know, I know, but they're gone now so let's concentrate. Where's the bloody safe?'

The two of them shook themselves out of their frozen positions and started to move about the cellar. In a corner under a basement window (which had been blacked out) Clive noticed a small black shiny box.

'There it is' he said. 'Let's get it open.'

The two of them knelt down beside the safe. Jon entered the code and the door flung open revealing a nest of diamond necklaces shining brightly from within a cardboard box.

'Are they real?' asked Clive.

Jon took a sample and eyed it with his magnifying glass.

'Yep – pure hundred per cent diamond. 'We're in the money' he began to sing.

'Right, let's get out of here.'

Jon packed the hoard in his rucksack while Clive fumbled about trying to find the bottom of the stairs. At last they found the first step and both of them clambered up as if their lives depended on it. They both emerged from the cellar to be greeted by a stocky giant who was standing bang in the middle of the kitchen.

'Hello my lovelies, hand me over the merchandise and I promise not to grass' said Grant O'Malley as he held out his hand for the bag of goodies.

'Not so fast Grant. We've put our heads on the line for you and we're fed up with being bossed about. You're taking the piss' said Jon.

'Yeah, you've been exploiting us for too long' said Clive and we've had enough.'

'Awe...very big talk Clive, where'd you learn such long words?'

'Enough of that O'Malley, we're taking at least half of these stones as we've done all your dirty work.'

'Is that so? Well, that's not the deal. I'll pay you of course but give me those diamonds now.'

Grant went to snatch the bag but Jon moved out of his way and as he did so smashed Grant's hand with his cosh. Grant screamed in agony as the two hurried past him. They made for the front door through the long hallway which gave Grant time to gather himself. He lurched towards them and grabbed them both by their collars and pulled them back with such force that they landed on the floor. Grant's hand was bleeding and the pain was excruciating, but that didn't stop him from kicking both of them in their stomachs and heads as they tried to get up from the floor. He could use his feet while holding his injured hand with his good one. There was a struggle. They all ended up in a huddle on the floor with Jon losing grip on his rucksack which fell to the ground allowing the diamond necklaces to spill over the laminated flooring. Grant forgot about his injured hand and punched Clive in the face. He let out a howl as he felt the pain spread through his hand and into his arm and shoulder. He recoiled and as he did so Jon plunged his knife into his leg. This made Grant more furious even though he was now damaged in two places. He wildly flung his fists in the direction of Jon but missed as he toppled over on to the floor.

'Let's leave him' cried Clive.

Jon gathered the necklaces and threw them into his rucksack. They both jumped over Grant's body but he wasn't done with yet. He grabbed Clive's ankle and twisted it with such force that he fell on the ground. Jon stopped in his tracks, turned round and saw Grant punching Clive in the stomach. Clive was shouting at him to stop but Grant, despite his pain, was relentless.

'Get off you bastard' Clive shouted.

Jon returned and attempted to smash his cosh on Grant's head. He didn't make good contact and Grant roared like a lion and turned his attention to Jon. He felt for his knife but it had gone in the struggle on the floor. Grant grabbed him by the neck with his good hand and Jon squealed like a pig. He shouted to Clive:

'Stop him for Christ's sake, he's killing me.'

Without thinking, Clive drew out his gun and shot Grant twice in the leg.

'You idiot, you've woken up the whole neighbourhood. Let's get out of here.'

Grant was writhing on the floor in agony. The last thing they heard him cry was 'give me back those f.....g diamonds'. But it was too late. Jon and Clive burst out of the front door and into their car. The whole neighbourhood was awake as lights were switched on in most of the houses in the immediate vicinity. Soon the whole place was lit up by blue flashing lights.

They drove towards Wandsworth with the idea of going through the city. When they reached the Thames, they chucked their weapons into the river. This was a stupid thing to do because it was low tide. The two of them didn't think that when it was light the weapons would be displayed like the TutanKhamun exhibit in the Cairo Museum!

Grant O'Malley was bleeding profusely. He'd passed out after the two villains had made their exit and when he awoke he saw two faces peer down at him. He recognised both of them.

'Let's get you to hospital' said Inspector Othman 'and then you can tell us all about it.'

'Stop this f.....g pain' he cried.

'Now now, Mr O'Malley, all in good time' said Inspector Francis. 'The medics are here and they will take care of you. We'll speak later when you've had time to recover.'

O'Malley closed his eyes and reached for his pocket. He managed to find a bit of screwed up paper which he handed to Othman. He beckoned him to come forward and whispered in his ear:

'Take this and find the two killers of Luke Masterson. I had nothing to do with his murder. You know who they are - Jon Smithson and Clive

Joseph – the same bastards who've done me over. Catch the c..ts. ' He then passed out.

The medics managed to stop the bleeding and got him on to a stretcher. The next minute he was waking up in hospital.

Othman unfolded the bit of paper and read out the registration number to an operative at the station.

'Identify this vehicle, track it down and get a couple of squad cars to apprehend the driver. Do it now.'

'Yes sir' said the operative who had only been in the job for a month but was 'keen as mustard.'

He then got in his car and made his way down to Charing Cross Hospital. He parked his car in the car park and displayed his police notice on the front windscreen. It began to rain. It was about 5 in the morning and he felt like a cup of coffee. He rushed towards the main entrance and was pleased to find a coffee machine in the foyer. He sat down, cup in hand, and pondered on the situation. All along he thought O'Malley was behind the Masterson killing but now he wasn't so sure. He was hoping that, with all his injuries, he would come clean and tell the whole story.

He approached reception but as he did so an elderly lady stopped him, smiled and asked whether she could help. Othman was a bit surprised by this confrontation but then noticed the volunteer badge displayed on her blouse. He explained that he was a police officer and wanted to speak to a patient who had recently arrived in A&E. She escorted him to the main desk and explained the situation to the receptionist. He was told that the hospital had no record of this patient and suggested he visit A&E explaining that he may not have been transferred to a ward. The volunteer offered to direct Othman and ended up taking him to the department herself. On their journey she couldn't stop talking, suggesting to Othman that she was probably a lonely 'old soul', her husband having died and her children having 'flown the nest.'

'You obviously enjoy doing your job?' he asked.

'I really love it dear even though I'm not paid. It's great to get away from the house.'

'Why's that?'

'Well my husband plays trumpet for a local jazz band and practices most days. You'd think at the age of 80 he wouldn't have the puff or the inclination, but he does and his practicing drives me mad.'

'Do you have any children?'

'Children? They're not children. They're both in their forties living at home. I can't get rid of them!'

'Oh, I see' said Othman realising that he had prejudged the whole situation! He reminded himself not to judge on appearances and circumstances until the facts were known – a basic rule in life which he had just broken!

She left him standing in the midst of chaos by the central work station where nurses and doctors attended to the information given out by computers while attempting to address the various problems presented by patients who had either been driven in by ambulance or had simply shown up in the A&E department. Despite the chaos it looked as though they were coping pretty well although at times a nurse or a doctor would exhibit a frown or an exasperated expression which was entirely understandable in the circumstances.

Othman noticed a nurse who seemed to have finished what he was doing and was calmly surveying the frantic scene before him. Othman took the initiative:

'Excuse me, do you have a patient called Grant O'Malley? He must've arrived early this morning?'

'Who are you sir?'

'Inspector Othman of the Metropolitan Police.'

'Wait a minute' said the nurse as he checked his computer screen.

'Ah yes. Mr O'Malley. Here he is. He's in intensive care. You'd better go and see someone over there,' pointing to a door at the far end of the room.

'Thanks.'

Othman pressed the buzzer and after about a minute a friendly nurse released the door and asked what he wanted. Othman explained the situation in some detail while the nurse listened intently. He was just about to expand on his story when the nurse told him to wait. Within a few minutes a doctor, equipped with stethoscope, approached him.

'Who are you sir?'

Othman repeated his name and title.

'Do you have some form of identification please?'

Othman showed him his ID.

'I'm afraid Mr O'Malley passed away a few minutes ago.'

There was a pause as Othman tried to gather his thoughts.

'How? He was only shot in the leg.'

'Yes I know. He was recovering well. We'd stopped the bleeding and his blood pressure was stabilising.'

'What happened then?'

'He had a heart attack. We tried to resuscitate but couldn't get him back.'

'Was this attack related to his wounds?'

'Almost certainly but we cannot confirm such a connection at this stage. He may have inherited a degenerative heart condition which was going to produce an attack at any time – wounds or no wounds. On the other hand, it is probable that the trauma and blood loss gave rise to an attack which turned out to be so massive that it was impossible to revive him.'

'We will have to have a post mortem to establish the cause' said Othman. 'I'll get the forensic boys on the job. If the stabbings caused the attack which resulted in death we're talking about manslaughter or even murder... I don't know, but we'll need to find out pretty quickly. In normal circumstances, would his injuries have resulted in death?'

'It is highly unlikely, although, as I've said, the causes need to be investigated.'

'Right, does his next-of –kin know?'

'The wife and parents are being told as we speak.'

'Okay. I will probably want to talk to them – the sooner the better. The two villains who stabbed O'Malley are also responsible, we think, for a previous murder. Any light they can shed on his activities and associates will be absolutely essential.'

'Fine. Let me have your card if you've got one and I'll give you a call after I've spoken to them.'

'Thanks, but please doctor, don't hang about. As far as I'm concerned, this is a full blown murder enquiry.'

'Got it' the doctor said.

CHAPTER TWENTY-SIX

I t didn't take long for the police to track down the said vehicle and apprehend Jon and Clive. They were both driven down to HQ and slung in separate cells. They were given details of the duty solicitor and advised that her services were available if they wanted to use them. The bag of necklaces was retrieved and stored away in the station's safe. They were told that Inspectors Othman and Francis would be interviewing them later that day.

They had been arrested for theft and causing grievous bodily harm to one Grant O'Malley in the early hours of that morning. Both of them sat on their beds and studied the walls. Both of them knew the game was up. Both of them had decided that they would bring others down with them. This included O'Malley who'd arranged the burglary in the first place. What they didn't know was that O'Malley was dead.

Andrew Garnett phoned his wife Jess. He apologised for his behaviour and asked her to visit him. She reluctantly agreed. When she arrived the first thing he asked was whether she was going to pursue a case against him.

'I don't know Andrew. It's one thing you trying to strangle me – which is bad enough, but it's another if you've been involved in a murder.'

'But I haven't been involved in any murder. You know me Jess, I wouldn't have the stomach for that sort of thing.'

'So what do you want me to say?'

'Come back Jess. Please don't prosecute me. I know I was out of order.'

'And what about your little girlfriend. Are you still going to deny that you've been having an affair?

'No. You're right. I was having a little fling. But like you, it wasn't any kind of serious relationship.'

'Well, why did you go berserk when I tried to take the tissue away with me?'

'I was drunk and angry, I lost it. I admit that, but now we're even, can we give it another go?'

'You've certainly changed your tune. Last time you were all for getting rid of me?'

'I know, I know. But as you said, we've got to stick together for the sake of the kids if nothing else. We've got to give it another go.'

'Only if you've been totally honest about Luke's murder. Did you or did you not have any involvement?'

'Well, to be perfectly honest, I did say to those two who got beaten up by Luke that I would like him out the way.'

Jess's demeanour changed. She went red in the face and her lower lip began to tremble.

'You did what?'

'As I said, that I would like him out the way.'

'What, you mean murder him?'

'I didn't use those words Jess'

'Yes, but to a couple of lowlifes that's exactly what you meant.'

'I didn't want him dead. I just wanted to teach him a lesson.'

'Well, you certainly did that. Please don't tell me you paid these people to do this dirty work?'

'It wasn't just me. There were other people who wanted Luke to be punished.'

'Like who?'

'Well, he'd had other affairs besides yourself. There were others who wanted him out the way.'

'Like who Andrew. Tell me who. Our marriage depends on your honesty.'

'There's a builder who lives opposite the Mastersons. His partner had an affair with Luke and he, like me, was not best pleased.'

'When did he have this affair?'

'I don't know. All I know was that this builder, I think his name is Parks, Martin Parks, saw me tracking Luke and asked what I was doing. I told him and we kind of went into partnership.'

'In partnership for what?'

'As I've said, to rough up Luke. We had no intention of killing him. We just wanted to hurt him for all the hurt he'd caused us.'

'But he wasn't hurt was he Andrew. He was murdered.'

'Not by me Jess. I didn't sanction murder. Don't lay this on me. I didn't kill him.'

'No but you paid others to hurt him which ended up in murder?'

'That's not my fault. That wasn't the deal.'

'You'll have to tell this all to the police Andrew.'

'You must be joking. I'll be banged up as an accessory to murder. No way. It wasn't my fault Jess. You've got to believe me.'

'But you're withholding evidence. That's not right.'

'Yes, but you said I've got to be honest. I've told you everything. I now expect you to support me.

You're my wife. In any case, if you hadn't had that affair, we wouldn't be in this position now.'

'Don't use that as an argument. Nothing justifies violence or, worse still, murder.'

'I can't go to the police. My whole life will be ruined.'

'You should have thought about that before you got involved with those two criminals.'

'I know, I know. It was wrong but I don't have blood on my hands. I didn't kill Luke. Those two lowlifes did.'

'Put it this way Andrew. If you don't go to the police, I will.'

'You wouldn't Jess. After all the things I've done for you. You'd be nothing without me. I've paid for your lifestyle ever since I can remember. Is this how you're going to repay me...by grassing me up to the police?'

'I've got no choice. Our lives have changed. I've now accepted that fact. No more luxuries, no more coffee mornings, no more dinner parties – that good life is over with. You have to come clean with the police – otherwise our marriage is over'

Andrew thought about his predicament. He'd confessed to his wife in good faith, but that wasn't enough. She wanted more. She wasn't going to support him so what sort of wife was Jess? Not only did she have an affair but she now intends to betray him yet again. He'd been a slave to her for all their married life and, if truth be known, before that. She had used him like a puppet – he danced to her tune. He'd provided the home, the cars and all the other riches while she had frittered away money on clothes, coffee mornings and dinner parties – all for her own grandiose image. She never thought of him during this journey. The only time she'd shown any affection was when she got found out about her affair and realised she could lose everything. And what about the kids? She didn't care for them. He did all the work to support them. He cared for them and showed them love. She never had the time. And now she was going to report him to the police? No, that wouldn't happen. It can't happen... It won't happen.

'Well, are you going to the police like a man and take your punishment or are you going to cower in the corner like a frightened rat? This is what you normally do. You're no more than a cowardly rat – a piece of filth. It's your choice Andrew. For the first time in your miserable life, act like a man. At least Luke was manly- he turned me on. You've never turned me on. You're pathetic.' There followed a silence. 'Do you hear me Andrew' she said in a louder voice ' you're pathetic, pathetic, pathetic. A sad wimpish...'

Andrew hurled himself across the room and, once again, grabbed her by the throat.

'Let go, let go' she cried.

'Shut up, shut up shut the f..k up you vicious slut.'

'Please, please, I can't breathe.'

'Good, you'll never speak to me like that again'

Andrew was in a rage – he had completely lost it. He tightened his grip on Jess's windpipe as she fell to the floor with him on top of her. His legs straggled her torso. He squeezed and squeezed using all his strength. He was in a blind rage. Jess began to make gurgling sounds as she tried desperately to breathe. Her pallor went a light blue and her eyes looked up wards. Her hands had been pushing against Andrew's shoulders in a bid to get him off – but he was too strong. She released them and surrendered. Her legs jolted for a few seconds and then went into spasm. Her whole body shook and then settled into a resting position. Her eyes were wide open and staring into nothingness. She looked as white as the 'driven snow' with her mouth drooling and unable to contain a swollen tongue that hung to one side. Tears ran down from her eyes causing her mascara to run. Andrew felt for a pulse, but couldn't find one. Her heart had stopped, she wasn't breathing – she was dead.

He got up and looked at her body. He'd released himself from slavery he thought to himself. The police would understand if he were ever caught. Jess had provoked him beyond all reason. They would see that. Once he'd explained the situation they would accept the mitigating circumstances – she'd pushed him too far. But, he still had a chance to escape and be totally free. Olga would look after the kids until he'd found his feet. Failing that Jess's parents would take full responsibility. He had to get away. He now had to work fast in getting rid of the body. As soon as he'd done that he would phone his lover and make his getaway. She would understand. She never liked Jess in any case.

CHAPTER TWENTY-SEVEN

Othman and Lucy often bumped into each other at work but were able to keep their relationship under wraps - or so they thought. However, many people suspected that something was going on and gave them curious looks whenever they passed each other in the office or whenever they had a conversation. The other officers, especially the ladies, could tell that something was going on. The lovebirds saw each other at night about twice a week and were thinking of moving in together – their relationship having progressed to the stage whereby such a move felt right and natural.

Lucy had got involved in the Masterson case in the initial stages and had shown herself to be a very effective investigator. However, after some further enquiries, she had been taken off the case on a temporary basis to assist in another murder in the East End. That completed, she was returned to Othman who was more than happy to have her on the team. Nigel on the other hand had taken a few steps back to allow Othman more freedom to do things in his own way. As the governor had said, he only had a week to sort it out before being taken off the case – Nigel knew Othman liked a challenge and was quite content to let go of the reins to allow his old buddy to prove himself in his own way within this short time scale. Othman had two more days before the governor would intervene again. He had to wrap it up once and for all.

Othman and Lucy spent a pleasant evening down at the *Spotted Horse* before going back to Lucy's to spend the night. He wanted Lucy to be with him at the interviews tomorrow. Arrangements had been made to see O'Malley's wife and family in the morning and *tweedledum and tweedledee* in the afternoon.

'Just take notes Luce but if you want to jump in, be my guest.'

'That's fine Oth. I'll stay in the background to begin with, and see how it goes.'

'Okay. So let me summarise where we are: before O'Malley died he whispered in my ear that Jon Smithson and Clive Joseph murdered Masterson. He gave me a note with their registration number. It's pretty clear that O'Malley was behind the burglary in Chelsea but when he asked his boys to hand over the loot they refused and a fight ensued. Forensics and the medical boys are establishing whether his injuries brought on the fatal heart attack or whether he was prone to have an attack at any time. In all probability, they'll find a connection so it will be up to the judge to decide whether it's manslaughter or not. That's just about it. Unfortunately we can't speak to O'Malley but let's see what we can find out from his wife.'

'Like what?'

'I don't know for sure. But we've got to cover every angle. Don't forget, it's only O'Malley who's saying these things about his boys – they may simply deny everything or, more likely, act dumb under the instruction of the duty solicitor.'

'I suppose so. Is there anybody else in the frame?'

'Well, there's Andrew Garnett, Jessica's husband. According to her, he admitted being involved with these two hooligans but I can't see him killing anyone.'

'You just don't know Oth. He had a motive?'

'Yeah, but I can't see it. I suppose he may have arranged something at a price, but I can't see him being more than an accessory. Besides, he's denied everything.'

'Worth following up though?'

'Of course. But let's see what we can glean from the main suspects first. Who knows we might get a full confession?'

'I doubt it, though I'm happy to show off my expert cross examination skills?'

'Too right Luce – can't wait to see you at work.'

After a quick breakfast they made their way to O'Malley's house in Woodford. It would take them a couple of hours to get there if the roads were bad, so an early start was necessary. They weren't disappointed. The rain slowed the traffic considerably and the North Circular proved to be a disaster. They eventually arrived at a large house in the posh part of Woodford. There was plenty of space on the forecourt so Othman decided to park his car in front of the house. They got out the car and rang the door bell. After a few minutes a young but haggard face peered round the door:

'Yes?' she asked.

'Good morning Mrs O'Malley. I'm Chief Inspector Othman and this is officer Deakin. We're here to talk about your late husband, if you don't mind?'

'No. Come in.'

They walked into a rather grand hallway which led to the main reception room. It appeared to be beautifully furnished but when studying the decor in more detail Othman figured the furnishings were more for show than anything else. They were clean, tidy and stylish – but they were a little over the top and lacked a quality that Othman had become accustomed to. He immediately cursed himself for thinking like this, reminding himself that everybody had their own personal tastes, and to make a judgement of this nature was bordering on an arrogance which he didn't believe he had. He then realised he was not beyond this trait and cursed himself, once again, for being human.

'I am so sorry for your loss' Othman announced as he sat on the leather sofa.

The parents were sat on another sofa and were holding hands. Mr O'Malley was a big man displaying massive tattooed forearms. He was bald and, like his son, had no neck. His wife, by contrast was petite and mouse-like. She hadn't bothered with her hair that morning and her mascara had run from her eyes. She was probably quite a beauty 30 years ago, but now, like her daughter-in-law, she was haggard and beaten.

'Thank you' she said lifting her head so that she made eye contact with Othman.

Lucy sat next to Othman and produced a notebook which she dropped on the floor and apologised profusely. She didn't know why she apologised. She just thought that any mishap, no matter how small, was magnified in the quiet, sombre, depressing atmosphere she found herself in.

'I know it's a difficult time for all of you but we want to speak to you about two things.'

'What are they?' asked Mr O'Malley in a strong Dublin accent.

'Firstly, have you any idea who did this to Grant and, secondly, what do you know about his work, his mates and his general activities.'

'All I know about Grant was that he was a good son and looked after Linda' said Mrs O'Malley.

'Linda?' Lucy asked.

'Our daughter-in-law.'

'So can you tell me anything else?'

'We don't know anything else' Mr O'Malley said. 'We didn't know what he was up to at work – we never got involved. We haven't a clue who killed him and we don't know anything about his other activities. We know that he got himself into trouble with the law but he assured us it was nothing serious. We believed him. We had no reason not to. He was over 18 and we didn't want to interfere. We saw him at parties and family reunions but never pried into his affairs. He was a good son and looked after us.'

'What about you Linda, do you know anything?' asked Lucy.

'I know he had a good friend at work – Luke Masterson, and I know that Luke owed him money.

But he may have told you, on the night of Luke's death he was round here. My sister was also here, you can ask her, so he had nothing to do with his death. When he found out who killed him, he told me.'

'And what did he tell you?'

'That his other mates, Jon and Clive did it.'

'Did Grant pay them to do it?'

'No. As I said, he had nothing to do with it.'

'What else do you know about these two?' asked Lucy.

'Well, I might as well tell you since he's dead. Grant used to pay them money for doing little jobs.'

'What do you mean – little jobs?'

'I honestly don't know. Grant never involved me. I suppose they were little betting scams or something – may have even been drugs.'

'My son would never have got himself involved in drugs Linda – gambling and drinking perhaps – but never drugs' said Mrs O'Malley.

'You're probably right mum. As I said I never really got involved'

'Are you sure Linda?'

'Why should I lie?'

'Who do you think killed Grant?'

'I don't know. It could have been these two but why?'

Othman looked at the three of them who were clearly distraught. He pondered whether he should tell them the whole story as he saw it. It would certainly upset them for no real purpose. No matter what crimes Grant had committed, he was dead. He asked:

'What did you know about his general health. Did he have heart problems?'

'Yes' said Mrs O'Malley 'he had a degenerative heart condition which he'd inherited from his dad. Joe had a triple by-pass last year but, as you can see, he has recovered well.'

'Good' said Othman 'That's good news.'

'Why do you ask?'

'Well, your son died of a massive heart attack as you probably know. He was recovering from his stab wounds and was making good progress. But without warning he had an attack.'

'So, what are you saying?'

'Well, it's not really relevant to us -your poor son has died and there's nothing we can do about that. However, we need to establish whether these injuries, sustained at the hands of Jon and Clive, we believe, caused the attack or whether the attack was going to happen any way'

'What difference would that make?' asked Mr O'Malley.

'I'm not sure, but it could be the difference between a manslaughter charge and a deliberate murder charge.'

'I don't think it will make any difference' said Mr O'Malley. 'They'll get off with manslaughter – you'll see.'

'Maybe, maybe not, but whoever did this to your son is still out there. I promise you we will find and convict them.'

'Good' said Mrs O'Malley. 'I hope you catch them. But whatever you do, you can't bring back our son – that's all we really care about.'

'I understand' said Othman. 'Is there anything else you can tell us?'

'There's nothing to tell. We've told you everything' said Linda. 'We just want to be left alone. If you don't mind Inspector, we'd like you to go now. If we think of anything else, we'll tell you of course.'

'Thank you Linda' said Lucy handing over Othman's card. 'We will keep in touch.'

Othman and Lucy left the premises and made their way to the station.

'Why didn't you tell them that the suspects had been locked up?'

'I didn't want to raise their hopes Luce. Besides, at the moment they don't seem to be particularly bothered about who did it.'

'That's because they're still in shock. Give them a couple of weeks and they'll want revenge.'

'Maybe, maybe not. I think they know more then they're letting on.'

'Probably, and we may have to go back depending on what these two 'erberts' tell us' said Lucy.

CHAPTER TWENTY-EIGHT

Andrew Garnett had managed to get Jess's body into the boot of his car. Thankfully, there was a door leading from the kitchen to the garage so he didn't have to go outside. He didn't realise how difficult it was to place a body in a boot. First of all, the body was very heavy, made worse by the fact that his dear wife was dead. Secondly, it proved to be an awkward manoeuvre – with arms hanging down, head drooped and legs dangling - and thirdly, having drunk three very large whiskies, his head was all over the place rendering his balancing and co-ordinating skills obsolete. As a result it took him several attempts to negotiate her transference from the lounge to the kitchen, from the kitchen to the garage and then, finally, from the garage to the car boot. The latter manoeuvre proved to be the most demanding, especially as the effects of a fourth whisky took their toll on his ability to concentrate which, like the rest of his faculties, was diminishing at a great speed of knots.

Eventually, with one final heave he was able to get her upper body in the corner of the boot. This left her legs dangling over the rear bumper. If Olga were to return now, the game was up. Thank God he'd asked her and the children to spend time with his mother in Cobham. He had to have a rest so he slumped down at the rear of the car with only Jess's legs as company. He was in the transition state from feeling pissed to becoming totally legless – driving was out of the question. Even he knew that, despite his inebriation. He lurched for the half empty whisky bottle and took several gulps. Minutes later he was asleep.

Several hours later he came too. His head was pounding and he staggered to the bathroom where he was violently sick. He cuddled the loo for about half an hour and then fell back on the tiled floor cracking his head as he did so. He obviously went back to sleep for a good couple of hours because when he woke up the room was dark. He managed to stand up and poured himself a glass of water. He wobbled a bit and then found the headache pills in the cabinet. He swallowed three of these and made his way to the downstairs bedroom where he fell on the richly carpeted floor with a thump. He regained consciousness after only a couple of minutes and made his way towards the bed. He slumped on the pillows which were scattered all over the duvet and closed his eyes.

He awoke some hours later and noticed the time – 11 pm. He felt better but knew he would have to nurse a hangover for the next day or so – he was not used to drinking so much. And then he remembered Jess – he'd forgotten that he'd killed her and had tried to get her into the boot of his car! He must act quickly – he had to dispose of the body. But where? He couldn't waste any more time so decided to transport her to the common. He would bury her in a place he knew was isolated and rarely visited. By the time he'd sorted himself out it would be in the early hours of the morning, so no one would notice him. He reminded himself that he was now free from Jess's constant moaning and this thought alone motivated him towards his immediate goal – to select various garden forks and shovels from the garden shed. This he did and before long he was sitting in his car ready to operate the garage doors. The doors drew up and Andrew started the engine. He got to the forecourt and was just about to take a right when he realised that he'd forgotten something – the boot was still open and he hadn't dealt with Jess's legs - they could be dangling outside with her high heels still attached to her feet! He quickly got out the car and stared... the spectacle looked something like a scene from *The Munsters* movie! Andrew quickly gathered her legs and squashed them, with some force, into an available recess which made Jess take up the foetal position. He closed the boot, got back into his car, and tore off down the road heading for Wimbledon Common.

He must have gone through at least three red traffic lights but thought, at 1 in the morning, there wouldn't be many people about. He drove towards the golf club where he knew a little single track side road which would enable him to transfer the body to the secret place he had in mind. Just as he was slowing up he heard the sound of police sirens. He looked into his mirror and, to his horror, saw flashing blue lights. At that point he wished he'd not gone through red traffic lights. He stopped his car and closed his eyes. The two cars stopped behind him. Two officers got out their car. Andrew wound down the window:

'Could you step outside the car sir?'

Andrew held his breathe, gathered his thoughts and stood upright in front of the officer.

'Where are you going sir?'

'To be honest officer, I don't know. I'm trying to get to a friend's house but the post code she gave me has led me to the golf club.'

'That can sometimes happen sir. I take it then you're lost?'

'That's right officer. I think her house must be on the other side of the club, so if you'll excuse me I'll...'

'One moment sir, we'd like to ask you a few questions.'

Andrew froze. He was terrified. His time had come – he was doomed.

'Certainly sir. How can I help?'

'There's been a reported burglary, believed to have taken place at the golf club about an hour ago. You haven't seen anything suspicious have you?'

'No I haven't seen anybody.'

'Well, it happened about an hour ago so that's not surprising. Any way thank you for your help sir – you can go now.'

Andrew drew a sigh of relief making sure the officers didn't see his face. He got into his car and switched on the engine. Just as he was about to make a move, the officer shouted:

'Wait a minute sir.'

Andrew stopped the car and wound down his window. He poked his head out with an imploring look on his face – he couldn't help this expression – he was on the verge of complete surrender and breakdown!

'Your left light's not working sir. You'd better get that fixed first thing tomorrow.'

'Thank you officer – I will. Goodnight.'

'Oh, and another thing.'

'Yes?'

'if anything comes to mind regarding our enquiry – anything at all – you will call us won't you sir?'

'Of course officer.'

'Good. Then I'll say goodnight.'

As Andrew drove off, the officer took down the registration number and sent it through to HQ. A bit weird he thought, travelling this time in the morning and getting lost. Best check it out.

CHAPTER TWENTY-NINE

Meanwhile Othman and Lucy had arrived at the station where the two stooges had been banged up in separate cells. Before they undertook the interviews Othman checked the reports to see whether anything of interest had been revealed. To his delight work had already been undertaken by forensics with a confirmation that both their prints had been found on the necklaces. Furthermore Grant's DNA had been found on both their collars; his DNA on Jon's badly injured face and neck and, lastly, his DNA on Clive's flea-bitten socks! The boys and girls had done a great job in a very short space of time.

'Okay Luce. I'll handle this in my own way but if I hesitate, please help me out.'

'No problem. This is your one Oth so go for it.'

The two entered Jon's cell where he was sitting by a small table with the duty solicitor by his side. Othman and Lucy sat down opposite. Othman made the introductions and Lucy prepared the recording machine.

'Right Mr Smithson, where were you at 1 yesterday morning?'

'No comment.'

'Who was with you?'

'No Comment.'

'Were you burgling a house in Chelsea?'

'No comment?'

'Did you steal a bag of diamonds?'

'No comment'

'Do you know a person by the name of Grant O'Malley?'

'No comment'

'Did you stab and shoot him'

'No'

'Ah, the suspect speaks!'

'Did you try to kill him?'

'No.'

'Are you innocent in all this?'

'Of course I am.'

'Are you sure you don't won't to change your story? Your cooperation could save you a lot of time and pain.'

'You cannot threaten my client like that Inspector Othman' said the solicitor.

'Okay let me cut to the chase. Here's the evidence: you and your partner, Clive Joseph, stole a sack full of necklaces at the said address around 1 yesterday morning. We know this because your fingerprints are all over the necklaces.'

Jon looked at his solicitor in a hesitant way and she returned the look.

'Did you know this?' he asked.

'I have seen all the reports' the solicitor said.

'Okay. Getting back to the evidence. Your face is severely injured. The wounds have been analysed as you know. The experts have confirmed that you received this wound at the time of the theft and that the perpetrator was one Grant O'Malley.'

'How do you know this?'

'Grant's DNA is all over your face.'

'That only proves that Grant beat me up. He's the villain, not me.'

'What it proves to me is that you know Grant O'Malley. His DNA is all over your collar and, indeed, your neck. Your response of 'no comment' was, as far as I'm concerned, a blatant lie. What else have you lied about Mr Smithson?'

'You can't say that' said the solicitor. 'My client has not lied – he just decided not to answer your questions.'

'Then, in the absence of an answer, I must make up my own mind and, as I said, he's lying. Let's face it Mr Smithson, you did steal the necklaces and you were involved in a fight with O'Malley.'

'Okay, okay. We stole them. But O'Malley told us to. He arranged everything cos he knew the house owner. He told us that he would be away for the night. O'Malley gave us the keys. He authorised the whole thing.'

'Why did he want the necklaces?'

'I don't know. He needed the money because his mate owed him but couldn't pay up.'

'Luke Masterson you mean?'

'That's right.'

'So O'Malley got you to burgle the house in Chelsea. You have admitted this. What happened next?'

'We got his necklaces but wanted a better deal than O'Malley was willing to offer. When we came up from the cellar, he was standing there. He grabbed the necklaces and we fought.'

'Right, and O'Malley ended up being coshed, stabbed and shot... who did that Mr Smithson? O'Malley says it was you?'

'Well he's a liar?'

'Who else could it have been?'

'Dunno.'

'All fingers point to you and your cell mate. Where are the weapons?'

'There are no weapons.'

'You're wrong. O'Malley gave us your registration number. We tracked your car. You threw the weapons in the Thames.'

'Rubbish. I ain't saying another word.'

'You made a bad mistake Mr Smithson. We found the weapons and your DNA is all over them.'

'That's not true.'

'Tell that to the judge. The evidence is overwhelming.'

'Can I speak to my solicitor?'

'Of course you can. Switch the machine off Lucy.'

'Interview ended 3 pm.' she said.

Othman and Lucy went down to the canteen and had a cup of coffee. They were joined by the solicitor.

'My client wants to cooperate and admit to burglary and grievous bodily harm. He is asking whether, if he does give a full confession, whether you will recommend leniency in your submissions at court?'

'Of course not. I will simply make a statement that he confessed to his crimes and that he was remorseful. However, he hasn't shown any signs of remorse so far, so I'm expecting he will at some stage?'

'He will do, I assure you Inspector.'

Othman and Lucy returned to the cell.

'I'm waiting to hear what you've got to say for yourself Mr Smithson?'

'Alright. As I've said, we did do the job and we did end up stabbing and shooting O'Malley. I coshed and stabbed him. Clive shot him. It was all in self defence. He came at us like a bull in a china shop. I coshed him on the hand. He grabbed our collars and pulled us to the ground. He's got the strength of three men. He kicked both of us and smashed me in the face. I stabbed him in the leg. He then got hold of my throat and tried to throttle me. I told him to get off but he didn't move. I shouted to Clive to help me. Next thing I know, Clive shoots him in the leg. We made our getaway with the necklaces. That's it. As I said, it was more self defence than anything else. He was trying to kill me. Thankfully we only did damage to his legs so you can't pin anything else on us.'

'Oh I think I can Mr Smithson. You see O'Malley died some hours after you laid in with the weaponry. You and your mate now face a murder charge.'

'You're having me on. We only damaged his legs. How could he have died from that?'

'Loss of blood perhaps?'

'No, you're bluffing. He ain't dead.'

'Why would we lie about something like that. O'Malley is dead and you killed him.'

Jon stopped in his tracks. He looked at his solicitor who looked down towards her hands which were resting on the table. He was hoping for some response but didn't get one. There was a pause...

'We didn't mean to kill him. That's why we concentrated on his hands and legs. Besides, as I've said before, it was self defence.'

'That won't stand up. You were armed with serious weapons. He was completely unarmed. You embarked upon the burglary with every intention of using your cosh and knife Mr Smithson, otherwise you would've left them at home. This is not looking good for you or your mate so you better be truthful with me from now...you say you'd never intended to kill O'Malley? Well, I believe you. It's like you never intended to kill Luke Masterson - but you did.'

'Hold on Inspector' said the solicitor 'that's a completely different case and has nothing to do with why my clients are here. You cannot proceed on this basis. It would be unlawful.'

'Maybe so but I want an answer from Mr Smithson.'

'Say nothing' said the solicitor.

'No comment' said Smithson without thinking.

'So you don't deny it' said Lucy.

'Of course I deny it. I never had anything to do with Luke Masterson.

'We know from two sources that you did.'

'Who are they?'

'Well, O'Malley's dying words to me was that you and Clive were responsible for Luke's killing. He then gave me a crumpled bit of paper with your registration number on it.'

'So what?'

'Another source, Jessica Garnett, told me that her husband Andrew had admitted that he'd got himself involved with you. He saw you and your mate get beaten up by Masterson. He took you to the underground and offered you money to rough him up – to exact revenge as he was having an affair with Garnett's wife. You agreed and, as a consequence, murdered Masterson. That's two murders you're going to be charged with. What have you got to say for yourself?'

'Nothing. They're all lying. I've got alibis for that night. I'll deny everything.'

'Turn the machine off Lucy.'

The machine was turned off. Othman explained to Smithson that they had enough to charge him on two counts of murder. He accepted that there was no intent and he would make this point in his submissions. He also accepted that O'Malley had been behind the burglary while Andrew Garnett had been behind Masterson's murder. He would also throw in the fact that both he and Clive acted in self defence when trying to ward off O'Malley, although he could make no promises on how a judge would rule on such a defence. He suggested in the light of all this, they would get no more than 10 years, although, once again, he could make no promises.

'I would like to speak to my solicitor again.'

'Fine. We will give you five minutes.'

Othman and Lucy waited outside the cell but were called back within two minutes. Lucy turned the machine on.

'Okay, I admit that we did Masterson over. We didn't mean to kill him. That was not what we were asked to do. We were asked to rough him up. It was a mistake. We hit him too hard. We didn't know he was going to die. I feel sick at the thought of it. We were sure he was still moving when we left him. We thought we'd just knocked him out.'

'Did O'Malley ask you to rough him up?'

'No, he didn't know anything about it. He did tell us to beat Masterson up, but that was the first time when we got punished. He didn't pay us for that.'

'I'm not surprised.'

' He didn't ask us again.'

'Then who did?'

'Andrew Garnett.'

'Is it true that he paid you to do this job?'

'Yeah he paid us a tidy sum. He didn't want us to kill him though, and we didn't mean to.'

'Anything else?' Lucy asked.

'Yeah. Garnett also asked us to rough up his wife.'

'Who – Jessica Garnett?'

'Yeah, that's her name. She was going to the police so he wanted to put the frighteners on her. As it turned out it was a bit too late ... by the time he'd told us, she'd gone to the police.'

'Thank you Mr Smithson.'

'Interview completed 4.30 am' said Lucy.

Othman and Lucy left the room and gave each other a high five. He played back the tape to Nigel Francis and the Superintendant and was congratulated for his first arrest, interview and charge in the UK.

Both Jon and Clive were subsequently charged on three counts: murder, theft and grievous bodily harm, and looked forward to a long spell in prison. Funnily enough though, they didn't mind this punishment too much as they'd spent most of their lives behind bars in any case. On the plus side, of course, they would get fed on a regular basis; would have a bed to sleep in and could use the gym whenever they liked – happy days. In any event, a spell in prison, as far as they were concerned, would beat being looked after by a nagging mother in Milton Keynes - every time!

As the meeting finished an officer burst through the door holding a piece of paper in his hands.

'Sorry gov, but I think I've got something important.'

'What's that?' she asked.

'It's a registration number of the car owned by Andrew Garnett.'

'And?'

'Well a squad car stopped him in the early hours of this morning. They were investigating a burglary which happened about an hour before.'

'Get to the point officer.'

'Sorry gov. They passed his number to us and we identified the driver. This is the same guy who assaulted his wife, although she never pressed charges. The officers felt he was acting suspiciously although never followed it up. They didn't really have anything to hang him on. Seems to me that we ought to be checking out this Garnett fella pretty fast.'

'You're right officer, although I don't think much of the officers on the ground. You'd better get over there right away Inspector. In fact all three of you go.'

CHAPTER THIRTY

Andrew Garnett had driven back home after his encounter with the police. He had had a lucky escape! He would have to rethink his strategy. Jess was still in the boot and the sooner he disposed of the body, the better. He quickly concluded that it wasn't so easy to dispose of a corpse and mentally ran through the options – burning, chopping, burying or dumping. Which was it to be? He'd better act fast because Olga would be returning with the kids today and enquiring about their mother.

He looked at himself in the mirror. He'd become old in a very short space of time. He had dark circles under his eyes and his skin had become a little more wrinkled. He looked decidedly ill which had resulted, he thought from the amount of whisky he'd consumed the previous day. He looked thin and gaunt – not an attractive image, but one that he would have to live with for the rest of his life. He had murdered his wife! The realisation of what he'd done hit him like a thunderbolt. At the time, of course, his adrenaline was running high and, assisted by the alcohol, his feelings were ones of triumph and freedom. Things were different now. He had to get away, bury the body in the middle of nowhere and get back to normality. He quickly packed his overnight bag, left a note for Olga and returned to his car.

Meanwhile Othman had entered Andrew's road and was just about to turn into his drive when a large Bentley took off in the opposite direction.

'That must be Garnett' Nigel said 'Let's follow him – see what he does.'

'Okay, keep your heads down – don't want him seeing us.'

They kept a good distance away from the Bentley and, before long, it was obvious he was heading for the A3. Andrew hadn't noticed that a car was following him. He was too intent on reaching his destination and dumping the body. Having a dead corpse in the back of his car was unsettling and the sooner he could get rid of it the quicker he could get back home. His phone rang:

'Where are you?' asked the voice.

'Hi darling, I've had to go shopping. Will be about two hours.'

'Where on earth are you going to shop?'

'I'm going to Guildford to pick up some wine from a friend.'

'Okay. Don't be too long. I'll give you a call in a couple of hour's time.'

She hung up. Andrew accelerated. He wanted to get to Frensham Ponds as fast as he could. He took the Hog's Back, bypassed Farnham and headed for his chosen burial site. There were few people around when he arrived, which was pleasing because he knew of a track which went straight into a thick forest and didn't want anybody watching him. He would be able to take his car down this route even though no vehicles were allowed. He was becoming a desperate man – desperate to dispose of a corpse. His desperation forced him into actions he would not normally take. He knew his car would be totally unsuited to the track, but he had no choice. He wasn't thinking clearly but his panic produced the adrenaline which allowed him to operate, albeit, irrationally. He found the track and stopped the car. He got out and looked around – there was no one around. He broke the lock on the gate with his shovel, opened it and ignored the no entry sign. His luxurious car shook at every defect as it negotiated its way using a country track which hadn't been maintained for many years. Of course the weight in the boot made it even more difficult and he winced when he thought about the damage being done to his suspension. This, of course, was the least of his worries although, for some reason, he pondered on this thought rather than his dead wife in the boot!

After about a mile he stopped at the side of a dense wood. He went off track and drove into the wood, ensuring that he chose the wider spaces between the trees. After a couple of minutes he stopped and surveyed the ground. He spotted an ideal place to dig a hole in the middle of a ring of trees. It was like a small copse. He could tell by the lack of footprints that few, if any, people had ventured into this part of the forest. He got his shovel from the back of his car and began to dig. At first the earth moved easily but when he'd managed to dig about two feet down, the job became more difficult as the roots from neighbouring trees finally showed themselves and hampered his progress.

Andrew Garnett became frantic and the sweat was pouring off him. He worked like a mad man – grunting and groaning as he managed to cut through the many roots with the blade of his shovel. If he could make another couple of inches the hole would just about accommodate Jess – he would cover her up with foliage and leaves if parts of her body could still be seen. This was not going to be a deep grave, but Andrew was prepared to take the risk of eventual discovery. By that time he would be far away and untouchable – or so he thought. In any case, he'd had enough of this little adventure and just wanted to get away as fast as he could. His first thought now was for his own survival. Thoughts of his lover, and even his kids, took second place; as did his partners in crime who'd helped him finance the act of revenge on Masterson.

He finished digging and rested on his shovel. He listened to the sound of the forest. Apart from a few birds singing, it was very quiet. He couldn't hear any footsteps, voices or cars. 'Thank God', he said to himself as he looked towards the boot where his wife lay.

Othman had followed Andrew all the way to Frensham Ponds. When he'd ventured down the track the three of them got out the car and followed him on foot. This was achievable as the Bentley was only travelling at around 5 mph. This necessitated a steady jog which all three could manage.

They saw him turn his car into the forest and continued following him until he stopped by a small copse. They hid themselves in the bushes and waited. They all looked at each other in amazement when Andrew produced a shovel from the back seat. Their facial expressions indicated that they all knew what was going to happen next. They waited until the grave was dug. At this point Othman wanted to spring out but Nigel signalled to wait. They saw Andrew take the shovel and move towards the boot.

'Not yet' whispered Nigel.

Andrew opened the boot.

'Now' screamed Nigel and the three of them lurched towards Andrew.

They were not quick enough. Andrew swung round waving his shovel in a threatening way:

'Keep away or I'll kill you' he shouted like some maniac.

'Just keep calm Andrew. No one's going to get hurt if you keep calm.'

'I'm beyond calm – don't come near me. She deserved it – I couldn't stand it anymore – her constant moaning. And then she had an affair. After all my support, the damn bitch had an affair. I forgave her. I asked her back. I thought she'd changed but she hadn't – she called me a frightened rat – I couldn't take her insults any more...it was building up inside me. I killed her but I didn't mean to. I just wanted to hurt her. But now she's dead and I'm a free man.' His face lighted up in elation as he said these last few words.

'Just drop the shovel to the floor Andrew and we'll take care of everything else' said Othman.

'So you can arrest me? No way. Let me go'.

While Andrew's attention was focussed on Othman, Nigel pounced. Andrew was too quick – he had nothing to lose. He swung his shovel which caught Nigel full in the face. His nose and mouth were split open. He fell to the ground.

'Drop it' shouted Othman who drew out his gun. 'Drop it or I'll shoot.'

Andrew continued swinging his shovel missing Lucy's head by inches. He dived into the bushes, fell down, recovered and ran for the track.

'You look after Nigel Luce. I'll get Andrew.'

'Be careful Oth – he's totally lost it.'

Andrew continued to stagger through the undergrowth heading for the track. Othman chased him and made good progress – he was the younger and stronger of the two.

'Stop Andrew, there's no point.'

Andrew was running out of breath. He lurched towards the edge of the wood and stopped to gather his strength.

'Put the shovel down' Othman shouted.

Andrew ignored his request and stood firm facing Othman. Othman stopped running and confronted him.

'Put it down Andrew. You'll only make things worse.'

Andrew made out he was going to drop the shovel and paused for a few seconds while he looked down at the ground. He waited for effect. He then lifted his head and let out a screeching noise while charging Othman like a raging bull. He was hoping his deception had worked. But It hadn't. Othman shot Andrew who immediately dropped the shovel and fell to the ground. Fortunately, he'd been shot in the leg and, by luck, the bullet had missed the main artery – Andrew Garnett was not going to die.

Othman alerted the medics and forensics and before too long the forest was filled with people in white coats and green overalls.

Andrew and Nigel were transported to The Royal Surry Hospital with Othman and Lucy following the ambulance in their car. They left behind a scene which looked like something from a horror movie.

'I think you've cracked this one Oth.'

'I hope so Luce, but more to the point, I hope Nige is going to be alright. He took a massive hit to the face. I'd hate to lose a colleague, and a good one at that, on my first case in the UK.'

'I'm sure he'll be okay.'

'I hope so Luce.'

The next day Othman and Lucy visited Nigel in hospital before taking a statement from Andrew. Before going to the ward they had a cup of coffee in the reception area and discussed the case:

'So, quite simply, Garnett paid Jon and Clive to rough up Luke which ended up in murder - making him an accessory, and, after a row with his wife, went on to kill her.'

'Don't forget his attack on Nigel. That's grievous bodily harm you can add to the list.'

'That's right – what a mess. And it all started during a dinner party, Andrew thinking he could not possibly be implicated as he was at the house. In fact, I think, he was just about to announce that his wife was having an affair when poor old June, Luke's wife, got the phone call that he'd been killed. It all kicked off from there. I suppose revenge can be sweet but I think our friend Andrew has gone a little bit over the top on this one!'

'Too right. Have you got plans for any further reunions with your old uni mates?'

'No way. No more reunions or dinner parties for me. There's only one good thing that's come out of all this.'

'What's that Oth?'

'I get to keep my gorilla mask!'

'And what's so good about that?'

'It matches the rest of my hairy body – as well you know!'

EPILOGUE

Inspector Nigel Francis survived his ordeal although his face was badly scarred. His nose had been broken in two places; he had lost three teeth and his upper lip needed fifteen stitches. However, the good news was that he suffered no brain damage and so lived to fight another day. His injuries had left their mark but if truth be known, Nigel was rather proud of his scars and refused to visit a plastic surgeon.

Andrew Garnett survived his wounds but became severely depressed. At various interviews he admitted to paying money to Jon Smithson and Clive Joseph to 'rough up' Luke Masterson but was adamant that his instruction did not include murder. True, he wished to exact revenge, but did not want the man killed. However, a murder did take place and whether it was intentional or not was little comfort to June, his wife – a sentiment expressed several times by Othman during the various interviewing sessions. Andrew acknowledged this and was clearly remorseful about the whole thing.

He did indicate, however, that he was not the only one who wanted to hurt Luke, advising that there were two others who were prepared to contribute towards the payment.

'These people are also accessories and should be named' said Othman. 'Who are they?'

'I'm not prepared to tell you. What's the point? I was the one who instigated the attack – they just helped out with the costs.'

'Look Andrew, this whole thing looks bad for you whichever way you want to cut it. It certainly won't help your case if you withhold information from the police. Besides these people have broken the law in exactly the same way as you have – why should you go down and not them?'

'I don't look at it like that. As I've said, I was the one who started all this – I tracked Luke down and made the first contact with the killers – they just helped me out with the costs.'

'Are you going to tell me or not?'

Andrew thought for a moment. He knew Martin Parks was no good. Parks had told him how he'd laid into his partner when he found out she was having an affair with Luke. Andrew found him both uncouth and obnoxious. Yes, he thought to himself, why shouldn't he go down.

'Okay Inspector, I'll give you the name of one of the accomplices – Martin Parks. His partner had an affair with Luke and he was there when Luke beat up his killers. He spoke to me that night and we agreed we would pay these thugs to beat up Luke.'

'Okay thanks. And who was the other one?'

'I'm not going to say.'

'Why not?'

'I have my reasons.'

'Was it someone at the dinner party?'

'Certainly not.'

'Your last chance Andrew – who was it?'

'No one, forget it Inspector – I'm not going to say another word.'

'Okay, I'll leave it for now, but you're not doing yourself any favours by withholding evidence.'

'I know that. I've no more energy for this. Just get on with convicting me and let the judge decide on my sentence'

Othman got up and left Andrew's cell. He stopped in the corridor and looked round. Andrew was sitting on his bed with his head in his hands. He was truly a broken man.

Andrew Garnett was found guilty of the murder of his wife and of being an accessory to the murder of Luke Masterson. He was sentenced to 25 years in prison. After serving one year, he committed suicide.

⊶ ⊷

June Masterson had taken over the role of Jessica Garnett as organiser of the Wimbledon coffee set. After some months after the death of Jess she'd decided to phone the rest of the gang and arrange a meeting at their favourite cafe.

It was a sunny Saturday morning and the ladies had decided to meet at 11 am which gave them plenty of time for preparation. In Joy's case, however, she was more concerned about pulling weights in the gym than bothering about eye liner and lipstick. They all congregated at the same time and after hugs and kisses, they quietly drank their first cup of coffee with the odd bit of spoken trivia breaking up the silence. Joy was the first to speak about anything meaningful:

'How are you June my love. How are you coping?'

'Not very well Joy, thanks for asking. I'm still in shock as you can imagine. I miss Luke so much. Thank God for my job. I'm able to throw myself into work and, for a time, forget about the terrible things that have happened.'

'Me too' Martha said. 'I accept that I cannot begin to appreciate how you must feel June but I must say, the death of Jess has knocked me for six.'

'And me' said Joy. She was a bit over the top but I loved her dearly. I can't believe she's not around.'

'I know' said Martha. I loved her too. She was a character – difficult at times (they all laughed) but I miss her badly.'

'And Andrew, what about Andrew?' June asked?'

'What about him? He murdered his wife. I hope he rots in hell' said Joy.

'That's a bit harsh Joy' replied June. 'She did have an affair with my lovely Luke. He must have felt so hurt.'

'Yeah, but that doesn't justify murdering your wife' said Joy.

'Of course not, Jess was so lovely in her own peculiar way' said Martha 'but I did have a soft spot for Andrew. I could tell that he was being bullied by her.'

'Yes, I noticed that too. There were times when I felt very sorry for him. He was very supportive to me when Luke died.'

'I rather liked Andrew. He was quirky and funny. I guess he just lost it when he killed Jess' said Martha.

'He must have done' said Joy. 'But I have no sympathy for him. I wonder how he's coping in prison?'

'I dread to think said Martha. In fact it brings a tear to my eye when I think how that family has suffered.'

'What's happened to his kids?' asked June.

'I think Andrew's mum is looking after them' said Martha.

'How do you know that?'

'He told me – I can't remember when. I know they've been living with the grandparents for some time now. First it was with Jess's mum and then it was with Andrew's'.

'Well, we all have to move on now. We can't bring back Luke or Jess and there's not much we can do about that scumbag' said Joy.

June started crying.

'Oh I'm sorry June, I didn't mean to be so blunt.'

'I know' June snivelled 'Don't mind me. I just miss Luke so much. I think about him every day.'

'Of course you do' said Martha 'It's all part of the grieving process.'

'let's talk about something different' said Joy 'I'm thinking of having a dinner party next week and you two are invited.'

'Not in fancy dress I hope' said Martha.

'Of course not, but it will be a hoot. I'm inviting all my clients from the gym. There will be about ten of them – all shapes and sizes; male and female; mostly single. Who knows, you might find some of them quite attractive – especially if you like wealthy, successful men.'

'I certainly do. Looks are important but so is wealth' said Martha.

June started crying again:

'I'm sorry, I think I'll have to go. This is all a bit too much. I didn't know I was going to be like this. I hope you don't mind. I'll organise the next meeting.'

'Don't go' said Joy 'stay for another cup of coffee.'

'No, better not. I'll see you soon.'

June got up and walked towards the door.

'You will come to my party June?'

'I don't know Joy. I will see how I feel.'

June left the cafe and made her way home.

'Poor girl' said Martha 'I don't know how she's going to cope.'

It was 10 pm later that day and Martha was getting herself ready for bed. Her mother was looking after the kids as a special treat. She would have spoiled them rotten before tucking them into bed at around seven. She would have then read from one of their favourite books before turning off the lights and kissing them good night.

Martha switched the bed side lamp on and read the first two pages of a romantic novel she'd picked up at a local charity shop. She soon lost interest in the story so decided to get herself a glass of red wine thinking that this would ease her into a good night's sleep. She hadn't been sleeping well since Andrew had been arrested. She turned to look at the photograph of him taken some months ago while they were having their little fling. She thought they could have made a nice little life together. It was a pity that Jess was in the way. She didn't love Andrew. In fact she treated him like dirt. It was God's will that her life was taken – she deserved to go, the bitch. It was only right that Andrew and she could make a go of it. Who knows how their relationship would've developed. Perhaps they would've got married - God would've understood.

She thought it was a pity he was caught and arrested for Jess's murder and then, subsequently, became severely depressed while serving his sentence. That situation didn't rest well with Martha. It was all a bit too messy and, like Jess, she didn't do messy - that's one thing the two of them had in common.

June Masterson also had a soft spot for Andrew. Not in any kind of romantic way, but she rather liked his sense of humour and felt terribly sorry for him for having to put up with that sadistic self - centred cow of a wife. He'd been particularly supportive of her after he'd told her that Luke was having an affair with his wife. He used to keep her advised of his movements and activities. He even showed her the photograph of the two of them kissing on Wimbledon Common – how sweet of him.

And of course, when it came to funding the beating up of her husband, she was more than happy to oblige and liaised with her neighbour accordingly. In fact, she suggested, since it had all been arranged to take place during the dinner party, that the money go towards killing the bastard – no one would suspect her involvement and she had the perfect alibis, including, as she found out on the day, two police officers from the London Metropolitan Police. Andrew was dead against the idea, which showed what a kind man he was, but June thought it was a great opportunity to get rid of her unfaithful and treacherous husband -once and for all. As it turned out, Luke did get killed, which delighted her even further as she and her baby would benefit from a life insurance pay out equivalent to four times his basic salary –happy days!